T0113995

Praise for Janna Levin's

A MADMAN DREAMS OF *Turing Machines*

"Sparklingly clear prose. . . . A dazzling investigation of genius and insanity." —*Temple News*

"Undeniably compelling. . . . A detailed, intensely felt character study of two striking figures in the realms of mathematics and philosophy." —*Richmond Times-Dispatch*

"Janna Levin's compelling narrative artfully straddles the realms of fiction and nonfiction, allowing us to viscerally experience the tortured lives of two towering intellects—Gödel and Turing—while learning how each, in his own way, left a profound imprint on human thought."
—Brain Greene, author of *The Elegant Universe*

"A brainy novel rich in revelation." —*Bloomberg News*

"The poetically heightened language . . . the incantatory prose and the stylized metaphysical colloquy . . . make it clear that Levin's novel is no mere assemblage of biographical transcriptions." —*The New York Times Book Review*

"I love the contrast of Turing's mechanized view of the world with Gödel's more open-ended 'incompleteness.' *A Madman Dreams of Turing Machines* is a wonderfully imagined book."

—Alan Lightman, author of *Einstein's Dreams*

"Wildly addictive. . . . A paradox: a work of fiction that is essentially true."

—*Pages*

"Janna Levin is a gifted stylist, and with this compelling book she has transcended the category of scientists who write books to become simply one of our most interesting contemporary writers."

—Lee Smolin, author of *The Life of the Cosmos* and *Three Roads to Quantum Gravity*

"Levin constructs a fascinating tale. . . . What's most impressive here is the elegance and sympathy with which Levin creates the fictional universe that accommodates these men's mathematical principles, while at the same time mapping a mathematical universe in which fiction can thrive."

—*The Baltimore Sun*

Janna Levin

A MADMAN DREAMS OF *Turing Machines*

Janna Levin is a professor of physics and astronomy at Barnard College of Columbia University. She lives in New York City.

www.jannalevin.com

ALSO BY JANNA LEVIN

How the Universe Got Its Spots:
Diary of a Finite Time in a Finite Space

A MADMAN DREAMS OF *Turing Machines*

Janna Levin

Anchor Books
A Division of Random House, Inc.
New York

FIRST ANCHOR BOOKS EDITION, SEPTEMBER 2007

Copyright © 2006 by Janna Levin

All rights reserved. Published in the United States by Anchor Books, a division of Random House, Inc., New York, and in Canada by Random House of Canada Limited, Toronto. Originally published in hardcover in the United States by Alfred A. Knopf, a division of Random House, Inc., New York, in 2006.

Anchor Books and colophon are registered trademarks of Random House, Inc.

This is a work of fiction. Names, characters, places, and incidents either are the product of the author's imagination or are used fictitiously.

The Library of Congress has cataloged the Knopf edition as follows:
Levin, Janna.
A madman dreams of Turing machines / Janna Levin.—1st ed.
p. cm.
1. Gödel, Kurt—Fiction. 2. Turing, Alan Mathison, 1912–1954—Fiction.
3. Logicians—Fiction. 4. Mathematicians—Fiction. 5. Genius—Fiction.
6. Philosophy—Fiction. 7. Psychological fiction. I. Title.
PS3612.E9238M33 2006
813'.6—dc22 2005037124

Anchor ISBN: 978-1-4000-3240-2

Book design by Robert C. Olsson

www.anchorbooks.com

10 9 8 7

147028534

To my father

A MADMAN DREAMS OF TURING MACHINES

There is no beginning. I've tried to invent one but it was a lie and I don't want to be a liar. This story will end where it began, in the middle. A triangle or a circle. A closed loop with three points.

At one apex is a paranoid lunatic, at another is a lonesome outcast: Kurt Gödel, the greatest logician of many centuries; and Alan Turing, the brilliant code breaker and mathematician. Their genius is a testament to our own worth, an antidote to insignificance; and their bounteous flaws are luckless but seemingly natural complements, as though greatness can be doled out only with an equal measure of weakness.

These two people converge in history and diverge in belief. They act out lives that are only tangentially related and deaths that are written for each other, inverted reflections. They are both brilliantly original and outsiders. They are both loyal to reason and to truth. They are both besotted with mathematics.

But for all their devotion, mathematics is indifferent, unaltered by any of their dramas—Gödel's psychotic delusions, Turing's sexuality. One plus one will always be two. Their broken lives are mere anecdotes in the margins of their discoveries. But then their discoveries are evidence of our purpose, and their lives are parables on free will. Against indifference, I want to tell their stories.

Don't our stories matter?

I shouldn't even be here but some things you can only get to in the most awkward ways. Even if I tried to hide it, to lie, the truth is it's still me telling this story. The unsorted catalogue of biographical facts provides nothing without stories with their dents and omissions and sometimes outright lies to create meaning that just won't emerge from the debris of unassembled facts. Because some truths can never be proven by adhering to the rules. So this whole story about Truth is a Lie. The liar says, *This is a lie.*

I am that liar, the third and final point on the triangle, the weak link, the wobbling hinge, the misaligned vertex. I am meant to carry on from the previous point and give over to the next. But I don't know where to begin. I am standing on a street, in a city. I'm going to catch a train. There are people streaming in all directions and one old woman strolling. Will any of us be remembered? Do any of us matter?

This story about truth and logic leads to atheism and mysticism. To despair and suicide. To the future, our past. To the present. So here's a starting point as arbitrary as any because logic does not unfold in time. It exists forever into the past, dictating how the universe began; and forever into the future, our fate already written by the inescapable rules of logic. We can enforce chronology because the linearity of time helps; it gives us roles in the script, a place to start and to end. So here I start. In Vienna. It is the year 1931. This place is as good a place, this time as good a time, as any.

VIENNA, AUSTRIA. 1931

The scene is a coffeehouse. The Café Josephinum is a smell first, a stinging smell of roasted Turkish beans too heavy to waft on air and so waiting instead for the more powerful current of steam blown off the surface of boiling saucers fomenting to coffee. By merely snorting the vapors out of the air, patrons become overstimulated. The café appears in the brain as this delicious, muddy scent first, awaking a memory of the shifting room of mirrors second—the memory nearly as energetic as the actual sight of the room, which appears in the mind only third. The coffee is a fuel to power ideas. A fuel for the anxious hope that the harvest of art and words and logic will be the richest ever because only the most fecund season will see them through the siege of this terrible winter and the siege of that terrible war. Names are made and forgotten. Famous lines are penned, along with not so famous lines. Artists pay their debt with work that colors some walls while other walls fall into an appealing decrepitude. Outside, Vienna deteriorates and rejuvenates in swatches, a motley, poorly tended garden. From out here, the windows of the coffeehouse seem to protect the crowd inside from the elements and the tedium of any given day. Inside, they laugh and smoke and shout and argue and stare and whistle as the milky brew hardens to lace along the lip of their cups.

A group of scientists from the university begin to meet and throw their ideas into the mix with those of artists and novelists and visionaries who rebounded with mania from the depression that follows a nation's defeat. The few grow in number through invitation only. Slowly their members accumulate and concepts clump from the soup of ideas and take shape until the soup deserves a name, so they are called around Europe, and even as far as the United States, the Vienna Circle.

At the center of the Circle is a circle: a clean, round, white marble tabletop. They select the Café Josephinum precisely for this table. A pen is passed counterclockwise. The first mark is made, an equation applied directly to the tabletop, a slash of black ink across the marble, a mathematical sentence amid the splatters. They all read the equation, homing in on the meaning amid the disordered drops. Mathematics is visual not auditory. They argue with their voices but more pointedly with their pens. They stain the marble with rays of symbolic logic in juicy black pigment that very nearly washes away.

They collect here every Thursday evening to distill their ideas—to distinguish science from superstition. At stake is Everything. Reality. Meaning. Their lives. They have lost any tolerance for ineffectual and embroidered attitudes, for mysticism or metaphysics. That is putting it too dispassionately. They *hate* mysticism and metaphysics, religion and faith. They *loathe* them. They want to separate out truth. They feel, I imagine, the near hysteria of sensing it just there, just beyond the nub of their fingers at the end of arms stretched to their limits.

I'm standing there, looking 360 degrees around the table. Some of them stand out brighter than the others. They press forward and announce themselves. The mathematician Olga Hahn-Neurath is here. She has a small but valuable part to play in this script as does her husband, Otto Neurath, the oversized socialist. Most important, Moritz Schlick is here to form the acme and source of the Circle. Olga, whose blindness descended with the conclusion of an infection, smokes her cigar while Otto drinks lethal doses of caffeine and Moritz settles himself with a brush of his lapels. The participation of the others present today is less imperative. A circle can be approximated by a handful of discrete points and the others will not be counted. There are perhaps more significant members of the Circle over the years, but these are the people who glow in color against my grainy black-and-white image of history. A grainy, worn, poorly resolved, monochromatic picture of a still scene. I can make out details if I look the shot over carefully. Outside, a wind frozen in time burns the blurred faces of incidental pedestrians. Men pin their hats to their heads with hands gloved by wind-worn skin. Inside a grand mirror traps the window's images, a chunk of animated glass.

In a plain, dark wooden chair near the wall, almost hidden

behind the floral arm of an upholstered booth, caught in the energy and enthusiasm of that hopeful time as though caught in a sandstorm, is Kurt Gödel.

In 1931 he is a young man of twenty-five, his sharpest edges still hidden beneath the soft pulp of youth. He has just discovered his theorems. With pride and anxiety he brings with him this discovery. His almost, not-quite paradox, his twisted loop of reason, will be his assurance of immortality. An immortality of his soul or just his name? This question will be the subject of his madness. Can I assert that suprahuman longevity will apply only to his name? And barely even that. Even now that we live under the shadow of his discovery, his name is hardly known. His appellation denotes a theorem; he's an initial, not a man. Only here he is, a man in defense of his soul, in defense of truth, ready to alter the view of reality his friends have formulated on this marble table. He joins the Circle to tell the members that they are wrong, and he can prove it.

Gödel is taciturn, alone even in a crowd, back against the wall, looking out as though in the dark at the cinema. He is reticent but not unlikable. The attention with which his smooth hair, brushed back over his head away from his face, is creamed and tended hints at his strongest interest next to mathematics, namely women. His efforts often come to fruition, only adding to his mystery for a great many of the mathematicians around him. And while he has been known to show off a girlfriend or two, he keeps his real love a secret. His bruised apple, his sweet Adele.

There is something sweet about his face too, hidden as it is behind thick-rimmed goggle glasses, inverted binoculars, so that those who are drawn into a discussion of mathematics with him feel as though they are peering into a blurry distant horizon. The completely round black frames with a thick nosepiece have the effect of accentuating his eyes or replacing them with cartoon orbs—a physical manifestation of great metaphorical vision. They leave the suggestion, with anyone looking in, that all emphasis should be placed there on those sad windows or, more important, on the vast intellectual world that lies just beyond the focus of the binocular lenses.

He speaks only when spoken to and then only about mathematics. But his responses are stark and beautiful and the very few able to connect with him feel they have discovered an invaluable treasure. His sparse counsel is sought after and esteemed. This is a youth of impressive talent and intimidating strength. This is also a youth of impressive strangeness and intimidating weakness. Maybe he has no more weaknesses than the rest of us harbor, but his all seem so extreme—hypochondria, paranoia, schizophrenia. They are even more pronounced when laid alongside his incredible mental strengths. They appear as huge black voids, chunks taken out of an intensely shining star.

He is still all potential. The potential to be great, the potential to be mad. He will achieve both magnificently.

Everyone gathered on this Thursday, the rotating numbers accounting for some three dozen, believe in their very hearts that mathematics is unassailable. Gödel has come tonight to shatter their belief until all that is left are convincing pieces that when assembled erect a powerful monument to mathematics, but not an unassailable one—or at least not a complete one.

Gödel will prove that some truths live outside of logic and that we can't get there from here. Some people—people who probably distrust mathematics—are quick to claim that they knew all along that some truths are beyond mathematics. But they just didn't. They didn't *know* it. They didn't prove it.

Gödel didn't *believe* that truth would elude us. He *proved* that it would. He didn't invent a myth to conform to his prejudice of the world—at least not when it came to mathematics. He discovered his theorem as surely as if it was a rock he had dug up from the ground. He could pass it around the table and it would be as real as that rock. If anyone cared to, they could dig it up where he buried it and find it just the same. Look for it and you'll find it where he said it is, just off center from where you're staring. There are faint stars in the night sky that you can see, but only if you look to the side of where they shine. They burn too weakly or are too far away to be seen directly, even if you stare. But you *can* see them out of the corner of your eye because the cells on the periphery of your retina are more sensitive to light. Maybe truth is just like that. You can see it, but only out of the corner of your eye.

DORSET, ENGLAND. 1928

The scene is Sherborne boarding school for boys in Dorset. A sixteen-year-old boy lies in the grit and sawdust against the rough unfinished foundation below the floorboards of the dayroom at Westcott House. The boy under the floor is Alan Turing.

He isn't there by choice. It has already been a while since the sudden shoving and scrabbling and it went dark. The wooden boards slotted into place. The clean ominous clink. The weighty, fitted lid of a makeshift coffin. Turing buried alive. It's a transparent observation, but children always underestimate the menace of their weapons.

There is a window in time, no longer than it takes for a few wrought puffs of air to loosen dust clinging awkwardly to the underside of the floorboard, when the wood shifts a millimeter in response to his struggling. The force of several tangled arms pushing downward minus the force of one boy pushing upward. He isn't entirely weak, Turing. He is wiry and strong, with a sinewy musculature. He strains and shoves until desperation bellows out of him in a deeper register than his voice can ordinarily reach. While the sound, a bit of a horror really, makes some of them anxious, no one of the boys has the authority to stop the others and so, with a small pit of dread planted deep in the lining at the tops of their stomachs, they collaborate to drag the heavy old oak table into place, two legs on the loose board, two well anchored on firmer slats.

Maybe this is an initiation ceremony. He grasps at the possibility optimistically. He means no irony. He does not mean a symbolic initiation of a boy into manhood. He neither uses nor understands metaphors. He means literally. There is a precedent for this miscomprehension. During his first week at Sherborne in 1925, there was an official ceremony that culminated in the older boys roughly collecting his arms and legs so that he was disconnected from the ground and folded up until he fit snugly into a barrel. He was then kicked down the hall. Although the blows were delivered indirectly, the humiliation was delivered rather more directly. Not knowing what else to do, he gave himself over to the incident. He bounced along—quite good-naturedly all in all—with eyes focused on a sliver of space between buckled wooden bands. But he thought it was stupid. He thought it was probably really stupid.

This is stupid too. He knows it is. He wants to shriek, to curse them, but the epithets catch in his throat, rough as sticklebacks. The boards brutally press his face to the right, mashing his cheek, his arms, and his thighs, so every arrested move is agony. The blackness an additional defeat.

He panics. He chokes on his own saliva. He twists. He knots his toes. He clamps his legs. He shrieks—a squeal that reaches up high in pitch as it mounts into a waterless sob. Struggling is making it worse. This is claustrophobia. This is delirium. Dementia. Even as he gags and spits vomit, he wants to yield. But he can't relax, soften, surrender to the incident, be kicked down the hall in a wooden barrel. While he knows they are stupid, while he knows they are phonies, he also admits there are many things in the world he does not understand and, on occasion, it is better to confess this lack of knowledge of the world. On these occasions it is better to accept being trapped beneath the loose boards of Westcott House dayroom. But he can't.

His knees grind. His toes kink. His back seizes and he recoils with a hyena's laugh—not altogether uncharacteristic for Turing—such strange speech deserves a complementary laugh—but exaggerated, a high and serrated scream of a laugh. Alan's entire vocal instrumentation is unmanageable. It is a kind of aural deformity whose source is no doubt the extreme brain chemistry of the highly functioning autistic. His voice booms and bangs and halts and stalls. He modulates the pitch but never the rhythm or the tone. The language of intonation is missing. The cadence that makes a voice bearable and creates meaning is missing. His speech is the grating clatter of a child's spoon on a hard surface.

His overzealous volume and peculiar elocution sometimes come off as cheerful. This malfunction, along with the tendency to withdraw, leaves the masters of the school conflicted as to whether or not he is happy. When they correspond with Mrs. Turing, they try to structure their observations of her son into a poignant conclusion but bungle the job. Unable to temper their frustration they ultimately blurt, "Undeniably, he is not a normal boy." This much she knew.

Above the floorboards, the room becomes a cavity trapping his shrieking laughter until it dies off ominously. The boys try to show off their callousness by ignoring the cackling vibrato slicing their ears. While they continue to play an anomalously quiet game, the pit of dread is jostled and falls deep into the fertile gastrointestinal soil where it begins its life cycle. Will it fester as an ulcer, or blossom into rancid abnormal cells? That depends on how each chooses to tend that messy garden.

Turing can't see through the darkness. The blackness coats his open eyes, as do large salty dust grains so that his eyes burn and water but technically it doesn't amount to crying. That comes later, when his ordeal is over. Or at least this one skirmish in his lifelong ordeal—a life of loneliness, persecution, and depression, lightly salted with childish bouts of happiness. But it won't be a bad life all told and it will come to be laden with achievement and significance so great that even he never recognizes it.

This isn't an initiation ceremony. It is punishment. Punishment for looking right through them, for looking right inside them.

There are bolts of luminescence in the world. Hard, brilliant candies that crackle like jewels, fanning pointed rays of gold through an otherwise gray landscape. Sometimes Alan can see these splendors unaided. He finds them in the woods or sees them in the sky. Sometimes he has to distill them from ordinary rock with clumsy chemical experiments he executes poorly in his room but pursues with the devotion of an alchemist until they yield gold, or just iodine, or some other element with a rightful place in the periodic table. Sometimes he discovers them with his mind like the inverse trigonometric function that he managed to express as an infinite series of simpler algebraic forms. These are the best, these dazzling gems of his brain's relentless, systematic expeditions. The smells of his chemicals and their incendiary threat don't deter him, but others are irritated by the mess and complain. His pure mathematical discoveries have the advantage of privacy—splinters of truth broken through the skin of confusion, framed by pools of crimson that only he can see.

To Alan, this is the world: luminous boulders, a string of precious stones. He jumps from one to the next just barely able to balance above the murky sea of fakes and phonies. Their world of facial signals and false strides, social norms. Their indirect, dull universe of dishonesty and contests and artifice.

He is baffled and lost in the tangled, witty exchanges the other boys are learning—mechanisms that evade candor with the flourish of the middle class. Through the swirl of debris of human behavior, he gropes for truth; and if he finds it, he stares at truth's sparkle with a fidelity that offends the others. Annoyed, resentful, they kick the rocks up in his face, not knowing why he stares.

DORSET, 1928

His room has never been clean, much to his mother's frustration. She tries to show him, to demonstrate: "Look, Alan. Arrange your shirts in an orderly fashion." And there are instructions too. "Clean carefully at the join of the wall and the floor or neglect will yield a rich harvest of furry dust." She pats his jackets down in search of filthy handkerchiefs with the desperation of a mother searching her child's pockets for contraband. There are always so many dirty cloths that even she belches with disgust as she reaches in for those buried deepest, hence oldest. With a lick of her palm, she tries to train his hair and wipe down his dark complexion. Alan is her cause and she endures her frustration with patience and a confidence that falters only occasionally.

Either he doesn't understand how to clean or he doesn't care or, most flattering of all interpretations, he is too preoccupied with deep and complex distractions, the sanctity and purity of mathematics, the profound truth so completely immune to human stains that even his clumsy approach can't tarnish its luster. Probably he just does not understand what it means to be clean, both for personal hygiene and for social success. And so the dusty taste of the dayroom floor is familiar to him, if more intense in concentration.

Turing reached sixteen this summer and recently discovered hormones. The hormones do nothing for his high voice, filling it with adult strength but he's unable to retune it to a lower register. So his odd, hesitant, not-quite-stammer gains power instead of abating. The onset of his adolescent biochemistry heightens his sensitivity to the bristle of stiff hairs that climb in dark corners of his armpits. As if to embarrass him and reveal at a glance what lurks in his most private of areas, the hairs sparsely grass his greasy jaw—something dirty and sexual right there on his face. But he no more knows how to groom and organize this new manly growth than he knows how to groom the hair atop his head that stubbornly flops forward, a deep black fringe, or than he knows how to align the buttons with the buttonholes on his perpetually askew coat that covers his partially untucked shirt and loose off-kilter tie, a man-child's poorly tied noose around an ink-stained collar. He is a mess. A dirty mess.

Dirtiness hangs about him like a slightly sharp smell rising up people's noses until the word "dirty" rises in their minds—as it simultaneously rises in his own—a reminder of the adolescent sexuality that the others are already busy forgetting.

The sexual tension of Sherborne School for boys is manageable. Smutty comments and explosive wrestling are valves to regulate that tension and they work well enough—not perfectly, but fine, just fine. The boys get through. Most of them yearn for girls, long for soft downy bodies with the basest form of urgency they are ever to experience, and the desire will never be quenched in their lifetimes. They can never satiate that adolescent lust since they can never again conjure up quite the same desperation. But they manage, even if they are tightly wound. Then there's Turing. He never understands how to stand, how to talk, where to look, what to say. His innuendos, his leering stares. Bloody Turing. Like someone who leans over to whisper and when you lean in, licks your ear instead. That's Turing, forever trying to lick your ear.

He blames the broccoli for today's predicament. The broccoli on his plate put him in a state of great agitation in the dining hall. It was pungent and fractal with the texture of a small bush. He likes his food smooth. Lumpiness or random texture plunge him into anxiety. Plus the sour yellow green was very similar to the color of the pea soup. The soup was okay because it was smooth and thin as tea—the country's culinary habits have been inspired by the stringent rationing imposed during the Great War. This suits him. He likes his food diluted and weak. Uniform in flavor and limited in variety. Color confusion is an especially foul trick. If foods are to have the same color, they must taste the same. But the broccoli tasted nothing like the soup, though they were both bland. The broccoli was soft and mushy but shapely. The very thought revolting.

What he really wanted was an apple. The thin tea-pea soup followed by an apple. An apple is not smooth, but it is red, nowhere near sour yellow green, and it has this in its favor. An apple is also round. Some apples are as round as globes, lovely and geometric, the symmetry pierced by the stem, orienting the fruit to the north. He loves apples.

He could not invent a happy resolution to the broccoli. It sat unwanted on his plate, cold as old fish. Discarding the boiled veg uneaten wasn't easy. The masters were intolerant of wastefulness and the prefects would surely notice. So he was already at a great disadvantage when he sat down to dinner.

He never knew where to accompany his tray. He preferred to arrive early or late. If he was early then he could likely arrange the food on his plate in private. Sorting the hues and consistencies and hiding any real offenders to be disposed of later. If anyone joined him he would do so by choice and he would probably be an all right dinner companion. Not everyone hates him. Nobody hates him. Some of the boys just can't bear him, which is not at all the same thing. They often privately regret their assaults on old Turing but still find the urge hard to resist the next time around. If he arrived late, there would be less food on offer, his plate automatically streamlined. With less sorting required, he could eat quickly and alone.

Today there were few seats to choose from and none of those were isolated. It was a game of roulette. Which seat to choose? Sometimes all the boys looked the same, each wearing a rationed fleshy-pink face. This happened only when he panicked—he couldn't put face to name to character. And so he tossed himself into an empty seat as though tossing a shilling, leaving it to chance.

It wasn't too bad at first. The table was noisy with chatter as he concentrated on his tray and continued to deal with the broccoli crisis. In Alan's unique inner world, he imagined himself to be invisible, entirely unnoticeable. But to the boys at the table, it was impossible not to focus on him. He fretted over his vegetables with jerky movements while his own dandruff salted his soup. One by one they stopped talking and stopped smiling. For a full minute the few boys at the small table put down their implements and watched Alan's oblivious preparations for the accident about to happen. Later, none of them would be able to remember which one of them first stabbed Alan with Chris's name. But just like that, the collision began as Alan was forced to abandon the solution to the food groups and search for their eyes.

It's not exactly that Turing didn't know where to look. He didn't know *how* to look. He gawped. He stared. His eyes dilated and seemed to draw some essence out of his classmates. It felt as though he could look right through them. It felt as though he could look right into them. Even more offended by his blue-eyed gaze than they were by his obliviousness, they mocked him with the name. It was a sing-song accusation, a whine and a taunt: Christopher Morcom.

Chris is Alan's first, greatest, purest, entirely unrequited love. He is a class ahead of Alan in school and from another house. Although a year older he is slight of frame, with thin, delicate features that Alan loves to study furtively, praying Chris won't notice. This slender prettiness can be blamed, at least in part, on a frailty induced by chronic illness, induced in turn by a heavy white glass of thick cow's milk, a satisfying half-pint of milk crowned by a lovely warm froth, seemingly ordinary were it not for the contamination of bovine tuberculosis. There was nothing special about the day the milk was poured. There was nothing special about the glass his hands encircled, except a mildly unpleasant chill from a layer of condensation that struck his palms. The chill nowhere near shocking enough to ward him off the poisoned drink, and down his throat it slid, coating his upper lip innocently and his bowels rather less innocently. The cough developed quickly, adding timbre to his young voice and plaguing him with a coarse production of phlegm. Since then, the bacteria have procrastinated, sustaining the host out of simple laziness. Chris keeps his illness secret, leaving Alan to speculate as to the cause of his small frame and delicate appearance.

Chris offers Alan the only respite from his loneliness. A pretty blond boy, he is everything Turing is not. An easy success, naturally winning, polished, and lovely. Alan could be jealous of his scientific aptitude, his adept physical chemistry experiments, his knowledge of astronomy, his superior telescope, and his family's cultivation of scientific literacy as well as a sophistication in the arts. But instead he takes the only other route available—he loves him. He never confesses his love outright, although Chris must know that this odd classmate loves him. But then Chris is easy to love and he must know that too.

There was Alan, pushing at the fibrous trees of broccoli, unsure as to the identity of his dinner companions, unable to resolve their faces, not knowing who was with him or who was against him. When the taunt landed, he didn't protest, didn't defend himself, didn't resent the implication. He grinned. A grin of indulgence at the dirty allusion. Bloody Turing.

Although the shattering of his plate shocked him, he was relieved to see the broccoli go.

Under the floorboards, he is given time to consider his gaffe over dinner. As the minutes pass, powdery dust clumps in the steam of his nose and mouth. Although he can identify the sequence of events—the boiled veg, the chair, the name, the grin, the broken plate—he's still not quite sure what went wrong.

The housemaster, Mr. O'Hanlon, saw the four boys push together into Turing's room—or maybe there were three. The frenzied energy of their limbs sometimes made it seem as if there were double the number of boys in a given spot, and the similarity of the fit of their blue uniforms made it hard to get a clear count.

He was also on his way to Turing's room, having spotted a flicker above his barren windowsill from the quadrant outside Westcott House. "Turing's boiling up another witch's brew," he thought to himself and aimed his shoulders at the stairwell door, determined to disassemble yet another of Turing's crude alchemical laboratories.

Alan's windowsill is undecorated, as is the window frame, after last month when the standard-issue curtains caught the pointy tip of flame from a candle intended to heat the crystallized contents of a spoon, a crucial experimental procedure.

Turing admired the transient ribbons of blue, red, and yellow winding through the hottest core of flame as the candle grease vaporized and burned and curdled to smoke. When the curtains curled into a muddy horizontal yellow conflagration it was a glorious crescendo and he couldn't help but stop and watch for a bit before he nervously snuffed out the fire with the neck and shoulders of his own jacket. Ever since, the window has been left undressed.

This morning Mr. O'Hanlon had to soothe the sensibilities of another of Turing's instructors. Fanning the offending papers in the housemaster's face, Mr. Ross, the form-master, thrust forth the unambiguous evidence of Turing's misbehavior. "Algebra during religious instruction. He does algebra during religious instruction!" None of the staff quite know what to do with the peculiar child, how to reform his filthy habits, rescale the high pitch of his voice, align him with the codes and expectations of the school. Their frustration blunted by a measure of fondness, a few instructors ease his way through the jabs and criticisms of the others. It is the self-effacing humor and ungauged smile that earn him this occasional kindness, as well as the periodically intriguing facts that stick out from the litany of scientific data that he can unfurl. But today, somewhat exhausted and feeling morally bound, his form-master implored, "I cannot forgive the stupidity of his attitude towards sane discussion on the New Testament." The housemaster couldn't entirely disagree. And with that the decision to keep Turing back in his courses was made.

O'Hanlon, annoyed at his own twinge of affection for this hopeless misfit, watches unnoticed from the end of the hall as four boys, but maybe it is only three, disassemble the chemistry set for him. He hears the signs: the initial dull thud, the crush of glass, and then the tense quiet that accumulates around a confrontation. He hears the effort it takes for them to grab Alan, and stands impassively as they clench his struggling arms and legs and deftly usher him into the dayroom.

"Maybe they can show him something we cannot," he thinks, and pauses another moment to hear the table land on the loose floorboards, the resonance dampened by the insulation of Turing's body before O'Hanlon leaves the hall the way he entered.

It's true Turing was doing algebra during religious instruction, but they underestimate the strength of his faith. He was thinking about God and, clichéd as it sounds, about the soul. Where is God in 1+1=2?

Where is God?

If he suspends the glass above the flame, the brew will sizzle until one chemical interacts with another. The concoction will sizzle every time. Molecules colliding with increased energy, their behavior ruled by the laws of physics. *Ruled by the laws of physics.* The future, present, and past of every material object is subject to the laws of physics. The orbit of every celestial body, the fall of every drop of rain. His own body a collection of molecules. His desire a cauldron of hormones whose chemistry has just been scientifically documented. His brain a case of matter, blood, and bone.

But he feels direct experience of his own soul, his spirit. He cannot accept that as an aggregate of flesh, a clump of matter, that his future, past, and present are already determined by the laws of physics. He cannot crush out the intuition that he makes choices, influences the world with his mind and spirit. He cannot crush out his belief in God.

But it gnaws at him. Where is the spirit in 1 + 1?

He designs a paradigm that welds his belief in the spirit to his firm materialism. It is painful and flawed and he comes to regard the fusion with embarrassment. The bond won't hold.

The sparkle of his materialism versus the enticement of his spirituality. Which will win? Both have the power to beguile him. Even today he was hypnotized when nuggets of truth protruded from the mess. When he heard the others coming, the stampede a declaration of their hostile intent, deep down recognizing his punishment for this evening's dirty talk, even then, he couldn't help but stop and admire the ribbons of blue, red, and yellow as the candle grease vaporized and curdled to smoke.

Chris had shown him the reaction between solutions of iodates and sulfites. Holding the mixture in a clear beaker near his face, he watched Alan's response as the solution turned a bold blue, tinting Christopher's hair and deepening the hue of his eyes. To Alan it seemed the other way around, as though Chris's beautiful eyes had stained the beaker blue. Almost in sympathy with the ions in the tube, a chemical chain reaction, Turing's skin tone changed to pink and then an uneven red. Not exactly the response Chris had expected but if he knew the source of Alan's blushing, he spared his feelings. He dispersed any awkwardness by drawing attention to the theoretical problem of computing the rate of recombination of the ions. Alan seized on this line of defense and set about devising his own theory in the following weeks.

He often tries to re-create the moment when Chris's spirit seeped out of the portals of his eyes and infused the room, a stunning concentration of his soul trapped in the indigo liquid in the beaker. He knows the simple form of the chemicals and the rules of their combination, but he can't shake the force of the impression that Chris makes on him. He can't limit the experience to the confines of ordinary matter. In the privacy of his room, he re-creates the experiment, waiting for thirty seconds before the sudden rush of color tears through the fluid. While the process enhances the vibrancy of his memory of that moment, the color never quite strikes the peak hue it reached the time Chris held the tube suspended near his eyes. Where is the spirit in human cells and chemicals and glass?

Trapped as he is beneath wooden planks, he considers such questions and the effort to concentrate curbs his hysteria just slightly. Alan's left index finger was cut by broken glass in the scuffle. His knees bowed at the sight of the weak rivulet of his own blood. The others got the upper hand at the junction of this near faint and here he is under the floor, circulating his breath and thumbing the thin split in the skin along the outside of his finger. Where is the spirit in a few drops of lost blood? Did he lose some of his soul too?

Despite the blaring throb in his ears, he can catch the unmistakable lilt of Chris's voice, smothered through the planks of the floor, as he enters the dayroom. Even in his current ridiculous circumstances, he is gladdened by the sound and smiles broadly into the soot. He squirms more energetically but just as uselessly, and resists a rush of patent jealousy. In the natural preserves of his permanent innocence, Alan's jealousy never sours to contempt. This feeling only causes him to regret his slovenliness for the first time. He sees in Chris something he never imagined possible. He sees a person functioning in the world who is not a phony. He is awed and mystified that someone who can recognize the predictability of the motions of Jupiter's moons can also penetrate the social rules of Sherborne School. He has studied Chris's gently placed smile and inherent grace, and they have given him a new standard to consider.

Alan's filthy papers, soiled and illegible, are a minor act of defiance. He holds in his mind's eye stunning jewels of truth, cut flawlessly by logic's rules. To transcribe these gems for the benefit of his instructors is a pointless chore. But through Chris he sees another possibility. One he will never achieve. Skill combined with cultured charm. Insight merged with polished execution.

As they lean on the table above Alan, there is an exchange between Chris and one of the other boys. Alan wants to claw his way through the wood and nails and see if Chris is up for a game of chess. If only he could, Turing, covered in dirt and a very little bit of blood, would gladly clamber out of the floor without explaining the peculiar circumstances of his entrance, without resentment, and plead with Chris for a thoughtful game of chess.

During their last game Turing lost swiftly with an abysmal sequence of moves. He was searching for an algorithm to ensure board domination instead of adhering to the strategy of the moment. When Chris executed a move, deciding on the rook, Turing was flooded with a feeling of comfort—something like assurance because Chris *chose.* He exercised his free will and eliminated Turing's knight and Alan could see with his own eyes that he was free. The source of this will in the face of a scientific realism Turing knew to be true could only be the soul, could only be a manifestation of God. Where is God in 1+1=2? God is in our mind's recognition that 1+1=2.

But even as he felt the warmth of this revelation, something stuck in his head. Chris was following some instructions. He moved the rook forward four squares, respecting the pieces to the left and to the right, respecting the rules of the game. He followed rules.

Under the floor of Sherborne School for boys, Alan considers an alternative possibility—that he is not free. That the boys who trap him there are not free. That Chris is not free. Although he quickly breaks the trail of logic to follow instead his religious conviction, Alan's flawed faith cannot truly comfort him. Every second, every heartbeat, every breath brings anguish. The brutality of this poisonous hour will precipitate a depression of his mind and body so grave that he can't be sure he will ever fully rebound. For a time his cyanide experiments are replaced with prototypes for an inventively devised suicide attempt—elaborate contraptions involving apples, lovely round red apples, and a delicate sliver of wire to conduct electricity.

He does live for Chris. And his damaged beliefs do patch him through. But a germ of doubt is planted, as a seed of dread is planted among his bullies. How that germ spreads will depend on how he tends that messy garden. In the meantime, he struggles to protect his faith from the brittle stones of reality, frantic at the sound of the desk as it is dragged back to its rightful place, frantic at the feel of the underside of the floorboards as they lift in response to the pushing of his twisted face, hands, and shoulders. Chris has negotiated his release. Wildly springing from the dark hole, he retches and pants and squints as he acclimates to the light and watches the receding heels of his classmates as he emerges from the floor.

In his distress and confusion, he returns to his room, where he then collects what he trusts to be the most decisive data for the atemporal quality of the soul. He is filled with a terrifying experience of foreboding, a terrible presentiment of Chris's death, when all he sees is this: beneath his bare window a shattered glass beaker in a puddle of blue.

VIENNA, 1931

The three large rooms of Kurt's apartment were crowded with frigid air this morning but nearly empty of furniture, though what he owns is fine and reflects his mother's delicate taste, a palate he has not inherited. His mother, Marianne, came to Vienna to care for her Kurtele, to fix him a home and see that he ate. His diet was appalling. He complained about every morsel as though she were making him eat sand. But then he had always been a delicate boy with a lovely moon face, pretty like an owl, with sad blue rings around his eyes. He was not of this world, her youngest boy. His cleverness intimidated even her when he was so young he should have been skinning his knees in a game of chase with his brother but instead he skulked deep in the rooms of their home where the attrition of light was worst. And though she loved him beyond reason, she often didn't know how to engage him. So she cuddled him and fed him and mothered him with all she had.

As a child, Kurt was either anxiously clinging to his mother or effortlessly withdrawn. He played childhood games with intense concentration, stacking bricks and arranging model trains. Occasionally he caught his older brother's interest in board games with confusing moves that proved ingenious. If anything seemed odd then, it was only the peculiar silence of the two boys playing. It irritated his brother that Kurt would play alone just as contentedly and just as silently. He was deeply embedded in solitary fantasies while his real family drifted in and out of his invented reality, as easily as imaginary friends.

Marianne structured the rooms of his Viennese apartment with decent pieces, solving certain problems of the building's arrangement. Just as always, he would pretend to occupy himself with ordinary things, a newspaper or a book, an untouched coffee he placed like a prop, too far from his hand to be believable. She knew he was pretending for her sake and often watched him sitting in a wooden chair she wished he would discard, static as a figurine. He would need her forever, her precious Kurtele. Although the date of her return home to Brno arrived before she could complete the interior, she managed to establish a few key points that defined the rooms.

Last night, in his mother's absence, Adele warmed his fingers in her impossibly hot hands, kneading the frozen ache out of his knuckles. Wrapping him in a scratchy blanket, she left him momentarily to descend the many stairs into the stone cellar, a branch off a network of underground hallways connecting several buildings along the block. She leaned into the dingy alcove identified by his apartment number on the wall just above the opening. She pretended no delicacy as she fell onto one hand in the soot and grabbed at hunks of coal with the other, tossing the black blocks into a filthy sack until satisfied by the weight of the collection. She pounded her hands together to knock free the worst of the charcoal dust from between her fingers and then wiped them roughly on the coarse outside of the sack before flicking superficially at the front of her dress. Carrying the heft of coal in one arm, she found her way out of the dark hollow of the cellar.

Adele Thusnelda Porkert. That is the name her parents gave her, one she continues to use for the stage. She used to dream of dancing in the ballet and dance she did, past childhood and adolescence and on into years of definite adulthood. Her performances had strength and energy but a heaviness too, a clumsiness reminiscent of her name. She watched the elegance of girls with toes chiseled to points, their bones molded prettily into the shape of a pink satin shoe. They hung in the air with long, arched necks until the stage softly carried them along again. They were free and in flight and so, so pretty. She would rehearse the leaps in despair, banging one angry foot on the floor and with great force only to get less than a moment's disconnect from the ground, her front leg landing eons before she managed the lift of the back. In the end, she wasn't able to float free of the weight of the earth or of her class. Her own toes were buckled and knobbed by the cruel binding inside the deceptively delicate facade of the pink satin shoe. They looked horrid and arthritic and her limbs felt stocky and sexual as she spread them to their limits. She never did dance for the ballet. But dance she does—for a Viennese nightclub, Der Nachtfalter.

Ballet dancers have reputations little better than whores and Adele carries a bitter resentment for this on their behalf. It has often been quipped that any man could keep a ballerina's company for a couple of hundred crowns. Liars. The nightclub, however, is harder to defend, as the other girls aren't exactly chaste or demure. If they ever marry they are more likely to give a husband venereal disease than a child. Maybe she isn't so pure either, if forced to confess. After all, what business does she have here with Kurt? But it is hard not to enjoy something you are so good at, and she is very good at caring for him. As penitence since she met him, she fights the sexiness of her own performance, turning it alight only for him. The applause of the crowd replaced with the silence of this one.

This is how Adele made the young Mr. Gödel's acquaintance: He lived on the same street as she and her husband. She passed him most days and though they almost exchanged looks (one would turn away before the other glanced) she hadn't given him much thought. When, on an otherwise average Monday, she dropped a collection of bills on the *Strasse,* Kurt was there to collect the fan of envelopes and ask her to coffee. Adele would not ordinarily have agreed. She's very defensive on this point whenever she recounts the story of their meeting. She is always offended by the presumption of men who approach her at the nightclub. But Kurt's invitation was something else entirely. He was unassuming and gentle. His smile was generous and contagious and he had a decided elegance about him. His clothes were handsome and he wore a hat well, marks of a real gentleman. He was so gracious, even humble, that it would have felt rude to refuse. More than this, she worried it would have seemed lower-class to refuse, like refusing to have a door held open. As he continued to carry her post to their destination he seemed attentive, potentially even adoring. He immediately made her feel—she's reluctant to add this observation when she tells it—more refined.

Over the cups and saucers, the crumbling cake, and the din of the café, he was warm and funny, interjecting now and again with just the right emphasis, while she filled the hour of their first assignation with her copious chatter.

As she began their relationship, so she intended to go on. Last night, she punctured any bubble of quiet that happened to drift by with the sharp end of the first thing that came into her head. The assault was quickly followed by a volley of reiterations, redundancies, and reinforcements. She gossiped about the other girls at Der Nachtfalter, savoring in particular the tale of the new girl with a predicament gestating. As she talked, she built a shapely mound of coals topped with generous handfuls of crinkled yellowed paper in the main oven and set the structure alight.

"Adele, please," he whined from his seat in the kitchen, "what are you doing?"

"Making you comfortable."

"Toxic gas makes me rather uncomfortable. A chest full of smoke can cause inflammation of the lungs resulting in suffocation. The metal content produces blisters and damages the heart tissues."

"Shush. Don't be silly. This coal is pure enough. The chimney is clear. I checked it myself." Her stubbornness was not unusual. Neither was his.

She knew he hated to touch the coals. He would rather freeze to death than light the built-in ovens that heated his apartment. If it weren't for her, he'd not only freeze, he'd starve. She'd find him here, a skeleton of crisp ice wrapped in wool. It would take hours for the frost to evaporate and for the place to have a chance at warmth, but before she would leave for her own home and the disappointment that was her husband, she would sift the coals, test the shoots, and clean any soot that gathered near the edges. By midnight he should be outright warm. If she couldn't be here to ease his waking and cook him breakfast, at the least she could protect him from the deep bite of the soulless cold of morning.

As she stacked—with her bare hands—poisonous aggregates of arsenic, lead, and mercury, he was stung by the possibility that she might actually kill him. Maybe by accident. Maybe by intention. The blue haze of burned fuel could have choked the life out of the apartment and soaked into the broth, baking the apple as it saturated the fruit flesh with toxic minerals. The fumes could soften, then twist the bones, leaving him crippled, yellowing his teeth, stinging his eyes blind. He tried not to swallow a deep lungful of air and concentrated on short sharp exhalations. He would not have survived the night in there alone, asphyxiated by the pollution billowing black as death from his brick furnace. By morning he would have flourished a cancer of sores, knocked dead by a crippled heart. He brooded quietly over these possibilities, indulging in a heartbreak that he knew was still only hypothetical. She had warmed him, dried him, and listened to him. She even sang to him. His gratitude was dense with affection before she insisted on the coal, drowning out his protests with "tsk's" and "shush's."

Her hands were filthy—caked with black dust. The poisonous metals could break through the skin that sealed her blood and guts, protecting her from contamination. The arsenic alone could bubble into open sores that spread like the rot. She was killing herself too.

When the fire held strong and she felt sure the coals would burn steadily, she sealed the furnace shut behind the small metal door, tended the second furnace in the far room with equal competence, scrubbed her hands clean, and set about preparing Kurt's dinner. He watched closely as she washed, feathering her slippery fingers together to dislodge particles from the webby skin between digits. He needed to be sure no fatal flecks of coal were seasoning the soup of potatoes and barley.

After she produced an apple from her bag and placed it on the table, after the potatoes were washed and sliced, and after the barley was soaked, Adele gathered her bag and fingered her hair smooth. She announced her departure with a motherly stroke of his hair. Using her full open palm, she followed the shape of his head to cradle his neck as she kissed him heavily on his cool lips.

As the door closed behind her, Gödel threw the poisoned

apple in the rubbish, extinguished the furnaces with the soup, his nose pinched in the crease of his bent arm, eyes squinted against the sizzle that spewed from the rapid cooling of the hot coals, until he made it to the window, hanging raggedly out the frame gasping for his life in the stunning cold of the fresh air. When he woke this morning, it was bone-snapping cold. And he was alive.

Adele has a stain the color of a dark port infusing the skin of her left cheek. The hue of her birthmark forecasts moods, blushing deeply in carnal moments that she is relieved pass quickly and positively scalding when rage burns her from the inside out.

She often studies herself in the mirror, striking just the right angle to hide the mark from her reflection. Her father, a photographer, taught her how to pose for cameras, and together she and he doted on the prettiness of the perfect, fair side of her face recorded in black-and-white on the final print, as though it were another child altogether that they admired. If no photographs could catch the purple color out of shadow, maybe her life could be remembered without it—a blemish like a bruise inherited from a mother she realized might be the littlest bit vulgar. She repeated the strange ritual with her husband, also a photographer, posing in near profile, her left eye, cheek, and lip occulted, and together he and she doted on the prettiness of the perfect, fair side of her face, as though it were another woman altogether that they admired.

A few weeks ago, as Adele dressed for work, her mother visited her cramped flat to crowd it even more with a harsh gas of words, advice, and criticism. Adele aligned her right cheek with the plane of the mirror to contemplate the woman she was not. Her mother wedged herself between Adele and the mirror in order to study the reflection too. There they stood, slightly staggered. Adele pinned up her hair as her mother left a faint mist of spit on the glass with her gossip. As she tucked and tugged and pulled at the loose strands in front of her eyes, behind her ears, at the nape of her neck, she noticed her mother do the same. Tuck, tug, pull, they fingered their hair in unison. Even as Adele slowed down to break the synchronization, her mother slowed too as though the change in tempo were part of the choreography.

Looking at her mother, the thick sagging jowls and carved line surrounding the lips, she knew she was looking at her true reflection. The plodding passage of time revealed its malleability and allowed her to step across the decades. She saw her fate clearly and with a weary puff accepted it. Facing her image in the mirror, stain and all, she thought, "I'm an old tart with not much time left." She knew then, and she knows now, that it won't be long before she packs her things and leaves her husband. That is the day she will become her mother, and Gödel's mother too. It is a role in which she will excel. She will mother him right out from under Kurt's real mummy, Marianne.

Naturally Marianne hates her. A dancer, nonsense, more like a prostitute to a middle-class eye and rather as bad to a mother's. Not to mention the age. Or the husband. Gödel's mother used to imagine that purple birthmark *was* port, or something cheaper, a viscous booze slipping down her cheek. Marianne would like to have been the one to throw it in her face.

What's more, Adele talks an ocean. She can't not talk. She can't bear an empty moment, what, when it could be alive with zest? She is vigilant in her offense against silence. She tries to unclutter her mind by freeing every thought that presses forward. Better to have all her thoughts outside her head and not inside. What's so good about a head full of thoughts? Look at Kurt. Inside they can irritate, become infected like a sour tooth or a dirty splinter.

Kurt has noticed she tends to get snared on moral judgments at key plot points in the gossip she relays to him about the other girls in the cabaret—narratives he suspects she embellishes to fuel her condemnation and fluff her own convictions. But she fills the air with harmless words and themes much as a radio would and thereby creates for him a background landscape of white noise. Adele never demands of him any actual conversation. She seems to understand that she is there to keep time and drown out the alarm of more individuated noises. The clink of a pin drop that can fray his nerves, the grinding of gravel beneath the weight of a man on the street, the spike of a dulled conversation as a couple pass beneath his window over Langegasse, the mounting pitch of the conspiratorial exchange as they approach. The splatter of noises leaves him strained and frightened. Her voluble puttering around his apartment smoothes out the clamor of the city like a dull blanket evening out the thermal eddies.

To Kurt, Adele is like a lump of earth come to life. No tricks or embellishments, no flirting with the rules, no violations of the principles of logic. In her simple uncultured manner, she is reassuring and clear, transparent and real. His beautiful bruised apple, his sweet little Adele. She is a chunk of flesh, real as mud. Adele is *real.* Her only extravagance is an occasional psychic episode, an incidental plucking of information or a subtle perception beyond the ordinary senses—a modicum of ESP. It is this filament of talent that Kurt turned to last night in his colossal panic.

And though the evening ended with the destruction of fires she had built and the dinner she had cooked, it began well enough because Adele was there for him, as she always would be, with a warm blanket, a comforting cluck, and a mothering tone.

The iron frame of Kurt's bed was a brutal conductor of the chill singeing his hand so sharply as he hoisted himself awake this morning that it might as well have left a burn, and the cloud of condensation that escaped from his damp mouth could have been smoke. He prepared for his discussion with the Circle most of the day and took care to present himself well. He applied layers of clothes like a dressing over a wound, carefully wrapping his limbs in strong woolen weaves. The third pair of pants buttoned easily over the inner two layers with just the right amount of resistance. He made sure the two pairs of trousers he wore closest were slightly short and stayed well hidden behind the cuff of the outer suit. A similar procedure was followed for his upper half—a series of shirts and vests created a padding five garments thick. Even then he looked lean although less alarmingly so.

Despite his detachment, his family's sophistication was not

entirely lost on him and surfaced in the subtle choices he made, if not in the few kitsch objects he clashed against his mother's design in the interior of his large flat, then at least it showed in the many garments that he now used to flatter himself, a reference to the rich textiles manufactured in his father's factories. He applied the finely woven jacket that still hung loosely from the line connecting the points of his two shoulders, and finally a handsome overcoat was draped over that.

Gödel loves these Thursday nights. The rest of the week is spent in near complete isolation, sometimes losing the sense of days. Comforted by the darkest hours when his loneliness is assured, he manipulates logical symbols into a flawless sequence, generating theorem after theorem in his notebooks. He fills the plain paper books with mathematical proofs that lead to new ideas that spawn new results. He can't always find a context for the proliferation of logical conclusions other than the pages themselves, which are covered on one side from left to right until the book is finished and he moves back through the volume covering the backs of the pages from right to left. In these ordinary brown notebooks he builds a logical cosmos of his own in which the private ideas are nested, his secret gems. His most precious insights he transcribes in Gabelsberger, an obsolete form of German shorthand he was taught as a schoolboy and is sure no one else remembers.

While he often loses Monday easily and tries to find root in Tuesday, and although Wednesday is a mere link between nights, he always knows Thursday. He likes to arrive early and choose the same place each time, a dark wooden chair near the wall, almost hidden behind the floral arm of an upholstered booth, not too close to the center but not too far out where it might become crowded, people pressing in to warm themselves against the heat of argument emanating from the core. Comfortably still, with an undisturbed tepid coffee he never intends to drink, he listens to the debates, the ideas, and the laughter, like a man marooned on an island tuning in to a distant radio broadcast. Proof that there are others out there. Proof that he is not alone. Proof.

He usually disagrees with them. Still, the Circle gives him a clear form to relate to, an external setting for his private cosmos—solid rocks of reality appearing in a fog of ghosts.

This evening he is later than usual. Knocked unsteady as he has been by recent events. He has his latest notebook with him, pressed against his jacket. His knuckles protrude from the spine of the book like barbed-wire lacings. The pages are nearly full, front and back covered; they must be read as a loop from the first page front to the last page back, then toward the first page again—a closed path, a broken triangle, and at the pointed tip a discovery. An incredible discovery. He is so impressed by the stream of symbols that accumulate particularly at the end point, where they began, that he feels light-headed, while his blood collects in pools about his bony knees.

He's in front of the glass doors of the Café Josephinum. Through the filter of the windowpanes the activity becomes an unreal smear of lights and colors. His hand on the door, it opens, that aroma, and he moves into the room. Through the filter of his eyes the activity persists, an unreal smear of lights and colors. Who here is real?

Pushing against a breeze of phantoms he moves toward the

table, pressing into a chair. Amazing that he looks composed. His physical condition is fragile. His emotional condition is fragile. He hides the former behind thick textile weaves and a well-manicured facade. He hides the latter behind the pattern of lights reflected off his glasses. On this stage provided by the Café Josephinum, he looks at ease, as though he belongs. But the past few days have been irregular at best. For one thing, Adele almost poisoned him. He woke into the hardest cold this morning as though breaking through the surface of a frozen lake and gasped for breath—the air shocking his nose and throat with brittle spikes of ice as his mind sucked in the progression of the past days. A terrible relief flooded his system and the relieved thoughts themselves confirmed to him that he was indeed alive. *I think therefore I am,* he thought. Both the thought and the condition of being alive amused him. While he has run the events over and over in his mind, they permute with each replay: an old woman, his death, then Adele who is kind until she dusts something into his stew. Then again: an old woman, his death, the rain, Adele manipulates his confession and blatantly builds a toxic pyre. An old woman. His death. The rain. Adele. Pretty, stained Adele. He aches with suspicion and the thick mucus of betrayal.

He also aches with disease. He is fatigued. His chest is sore. He has no breath. This very evening he coughed up blood. His heart has become stiff and scarred after a bout of rheumatic fever at the age of eight. A valve in his atrium fused and constricted over the years. It took the disease a full decade to declare the specific threat intended. He is plagued by attacks. A backwash of his blood stretches the chambers, depriving his arteries. He lives in constant fear for his life. Every minute framed by panic. The flutter in his chest a warning of a potential blood clot, suffocation, or heart failure. He shouldn't be here in the smoky air, warm and virulent. But the relief that filled his limbs this morning gave him a feeling of urgency and ambition. And he needs to see Moritz.

The Circle doesn't take shape until Moritz Schlick arrives. He enters like a gale, his entrance embellished by a curl of eddies in his wake that flow around the door and into the room. He is the chair of Philosophy of the Inductive Sciences at the university, a title that carries great prestige and authority. Moritz is always a gentleman, always gracious and earnest and admirable. As he rocks into a chair, hands are waved, more coffees are ordered, and in the darkening room, darker than the ebbing day, they all begin to settle amid clanking dishes, knocking elbows, their collective weight leveraged inward. The table wobbles as cups rise and fall and a circle forms.

It's Moritz Schlick's circle. Drawn together by his invitation and kept together by his soothing tones. They come here to orbit around truth, to throw off centuries of misguided faith, the shackles of religion, the hypnotism of metaphysics. They celebrate the heft of their own weight in a solid chair, the heat off the coffee, the sound their voices manufacture within the walls of the café. Some are delirious with the immediacy of this day because it is all that matters. There is nothing else. Everything true is summed up in the chair, the cup, the building. There is only pressure, heat, and force. *The world is all that is the case.*

Moritz knows the greatness that can emerge from the members he has chosen, so he smoothes the caustic edges between egos and makes out of them a collective, an eclectic orchestra created out of dissonance. Moritz is the glue that holds together the communist, the mathematician, the empiricist. He has selected each person here with care, patiently turning them over in his mind, studying them with his kind eyes. They are comforted by his self-assurance and are sincerely flattered by the invitation to Thursday's discussions, if they are ever fortunate enough to receive the summons. There are many for whom the hoped-for invitation never comes.

Gödel blushed with either vanity or shyness, who can know for sure, when Moritz approached him in the room in the basement of the mathematics institute and extended the invitation almost four years ago. Kurt was at the chalkboard organizing another student's thoughts in spare symbols, lovely dusty marks on a landscape of poorly erased predecessors. He always transcribes the skeleton in the pure notation of symbolic logic first and with such care before he begins to speak. Even though he was only a twenty-one-year-old student, the others watched with admiration for his ability to see through to the logical bones in their debates, like a chef skillfully removing the endoskeleton of a filleted fish without a morsel of clinging flesh. Moritz watched him too and moved by the lucidity of Gödel's resolution of a problem he himself had found distractingly difficult, he came to his final decision to extend to Kurt an invitation to his Circle on Thursday nights.

Moritz joined him at the board, quietly adding a fine comment on the infinite list of integers that branched off the middle rib of the fish's spine. And in this smooth manner he eased

Gödel into conversation. Everyone either knows by instinct or learns by plain experiment to meet Gödel with mathematics first. And so Moritz approached with the right words about infinity and integers and earned that look of gratitude and trust. As he shook Kurt's hand and his own head in grateful amazement, they talked.

"Herr Professor, I have been thinking about the Liar's Paradox where the liar says, *This sentence is false.*"

"Ah, the antinomy of the liar. Yes, that liar who says, *This sentence is false.*"

"The sentence cannot be false."

"Because if it is false as claimed, then it must be true. A contradiction." Studying his young student for a time Moritz stroked his lip dry and concluded his motion with the reply, "And it cannot be true. Because if it is true, then it is false which is again a contradiction. It is a paradox and an artifact of our careless use of language. Mathematics will never allow such a paradox. Mathematical propositions will either be true or false with no contradictions."

"What if mathematics is not free of such propositions?"

"It must be. Mathematics *must* be complete. There are no unsolvable problems."

Ever since that morning of the invitation and the antinomy of the liar, Gödel has found Moritz's very presence reassuring. If Kurt was different in character, more affectionate, less rigid; and if Moritz too were just a little different, more spontaneous, less reserved, Gödel could have come to love Moritz like a father. Instead he feels something more formal, more distant, more appropriate probably. He feels grateful. He keeps this feeling to himself, and the sentiment has almost no outward manifestation beyond his attendance here at Moritz's discussions. He believes that Moritz is real, that he exists, and his faith solidified the moment that Moritz shared the comment on the infinite list of numbers. With that insight, it was as though Moritz uttered a code word. *I am one of the real ones,* his comment certified, and with that he crystallized from the cloud and took shape.

This isn't every Thursday. This is one Thursday in particular. An evening on which Kurt is impatient to see him, on which the glass doors of the café swing wide and Moritz enters with a flourish of a curling breeze. He takes his place at the beginning and end of the Circle. The meeting begins as it always does. Moritz calls for silence as he strokes the articulated peaks of his top lip with his forefinger, looking deep into the nut-brown coffee in front of him. He is smiling to himself.

The others wait for Moritz to begin as a small quiet sphere emanates from the table and surrounds them, separates them from the clamor of the café. The youngest members of the Circle struggle in the spotlight the silence generates. They are ambitious. They are nervous. They are ready to argue and to revel. Although Gödel is quite different in temperament, he nevertheless feels as though he belongs here, that he is welcome, and it bathes him in a feeling closest to relief. Moritz makes all of this possible. He creates the silence, the spotlight, the scene. While a young new recruit swings the ankle of his crossed leg, Kurt looks to Herr Professor Moritz Schlick for an indication of the right moment to offer his discovery.

Moritz meanwhile pays Kurt no special attention. Like many of the others, Moritz is distracted by the experience of this single ordinary day. He feels how today has emerged as a bead on a strand of beads and how it will give over to the next in the sequence, another single great and ordinary day. Even as he begins to talk on the pristine platform of his friends' silence, he looks back over the loose knots along his trajectory and sees, as if flipping through a collection of pictures, the primary forces that brought him to this moment, to this table, to this circle. He sees how he got here from there.

The series of pictures that snap across Moritz's mind starts arbitrarily with German Uhlans in 1914. He watched them march out of Berlin and cheered the cavalry of sculptured metal helmets with a spike at the very crown, a weapon in itself. He watched boys he knew join the infantry and express satisfaction with their undecorated metal helmets, bald domes extending over their ears. They took comfort in restraints during a time of crisis and accepted the uniform that buttoned from navel to a tight collar about the throat, one button a nodule against the Adam's apple as they choked down rations of preserved meat and stale heavy bread. They marched out of Berlin cradling heavy guns in their hands balanced in the hollows of their shoulders and he never saw them again.

During his two years of war service, he calculated ballistic trajectories from a ditch of wet mud. As he watched a hole tear in his friend's flesh, the orbit of blood from another's severed jugular, the lifelessness of a stranger's broken spine, certain metaphysical notions drained out of his own wounds along with his comfort in the harness of his uniform. He noted the uselessness of his earlier scholarship against the crudest artillery. Faith, Metaphysics, Theology—impotent rhymes in the face of atrocity. Empty incantations that served up nothing, created nothing, built nothing. There were only bullets, trajectories, and wind. Physical, calculable, brutal.

His disappointment over the loss of his intellectual heritage was nearly as grave as the defeat of his nation. Still his antipathy remained polite although his dissatisfaction grew even as his wounds healed.

Then came Ludwig Wittgenstein, and Moritz's reserve burst under the incision made by these words: *The world is all that is the case.*

It is no surprise that in his review of the trajectory that brought him here, there are many images of Wittgenstein. The man mesmerizes anyone who comes near him, and he mesmerized Moritz. Wittgenstein is a philosopher, a great philosopher, and progeny of one of the most extravagantly wealthy and cultured families in Vienna, in fact, in all of Europe. Some people say he is the greatest philosopher of the twentieth century. *He* certainly thinks so. Members of the Circle obsess over his only book, the *Tractatus Logico-Philosophicus,* a series of logical proclamations, a polemic, each phrase exuded without explanation or defense so that it reads as though written in meter but a kind of stochastic meter. Sentence by sentence the members of the Circle went through the *Tractatus.* The second time took nearly a year.

Despite the implications of a numbering system that lends a biblical quality to the text, the document persistently lacks cohesion. But on closer reading the book impresses them one by one at first and then handful by handful until his ideas sit very near the epicenter of their thinking. A man with a rare and intoxicating personality, he rules them from afar and with near complete disinterest. He never comes to the Café Josephinum, perhaps only heightening their obsession with him, the intense desire fed on unrequited love.

Moritz is the only one Wittgenstein actually agrees to see in person. Their first meeting occurred at the home of Margarete, one of Wittgenstein's eight siblings, though suicide would eventually reduce their numbers to five. There he labored obsessively on the construction of her house in Kundmanngasse. First there was just the shape of Wittgenstein bent over a corner of the room, measuring a fitting. For a second he was just a man. But then he unfurled and twisted and lunged without actually moving. He lunged with his eyes. He looked unlike anyone Moritz had ever seen. The righteous nose, the gothic eyes, the frisson of wiry hair—bright, searching, and infectious. He seemed to be in a perpetual state of electrocution. The overall effect was to roast otherwise brilliant people—including Moritz—into fanatical, unwanted apostles. Of all the pictures of Wittgenstein in Moritz's mind, that moment they first stood face to face is the brightest.

As he slipped off to sleep the night of their initial meeting, Moritz was ecstatic, as though still glowing from the white-hot intensity of the full fire of the savior himself. As if in one motion Moritz rose from bed the next morning, stepped into his clothes and past the day, down the street, into Thursday evening and strode into the Café Josephinum while one sentence seared his mouth, the first line of the *Tractatus:*

1. The world is all that is the case.

In the commotion of the café, with his Circle to bear witness, Moritz, animated by an aberrant sarcasm and contempt, tore off the yoke of German metaphysics, ripping down notions like "The Absolute," "Spirit," and "God" and watched them vaporize before hitting the ground. Faith, Mysticism—it's not that these ideas are *false.* They are *meaningless.* Meaningless statements vying for the status of Truth. Pathetic contaminants fouling people's minds. A dissection was hardly needed once the cloak was ripped away; but he provided one anyway, bludgeoning the influential words, beating them into a lifeless pulp. There was no turning back to illusion and self-deception; and so here they are, a few years later, on a Thursday evening, charged and terrified by their victory, by Moritz's brutality. For better or worse, they have to trudge forward.

These images flicker past, a choppy movie of a few frames with the last one a crude sketch of this very moment as Moritz opens the table to discussion of facts of the world, of Wittgenstein, of Truth.

But this is why Kurt needs to be here. He must speak to Moritz, who brings them all together, who creates this place in which he can belong. His heart cramps. His mind cramps. The poison he can still taste pricks his swollen tongue. The ghosts. The visions. This is what he must tell Moritz, this: The world is *not* all that is the case.

At 5:02 yesterday evening, Kurt kept an appointment with a clairvoyant, a Gypsy, a medium—a very old woman in a very old red chair. The self-proclaimed Gypsies have recently wafted into Vienna like brightly colored leaves. They settled in nooks and corners, raked into groups that drift around the city in clusters. The sheer number of clairvoyants drew the attention of a legitimate study organized by professors at the university. The Romanian nomads, who are not at all of Egyptian descent despite stories of nobility and lost empires, bring claims of magic trinkets and extrasensory perception. Magic and spiritualism are the enemies of rational thinking and thereby have declared themselves Moritz's enemy. But a perversion of honesty persuaded some scholars to attend a séance or two with as open a mind to the fair evaluation of the proceedings as they could muster. They persuaded themselves to go with this simple argument: If only one man possessed the sense of smell and could thus detect a garden of lavender from the far side of a brick wall, all others would be amazed by his extrasensory perception, yet no magic would be involved whatsoever, just molecules carried on the air to the cells of the nose. Just basic physics, chemistry, and anatomy. If there was a physical process at work allowing some heightened perceptions, they would do their best to evaluate them. Kurt joined some of the earliest invitations to bear witness to the claims of a medium. As the evidence accumulated to confirm the others' suspicions of a hoax, in perfect contrast Kurt was completely convinced that the performance was real. Ever since, he has become an occasional patron of the various psychics around the city.

He finds these visits mildly unpleasant but necessary, much like a visit to the doctor. The news isn't always good. Last night's appointment was his first with the self-proclaimed Gypsy Queen. She had a good reputation as well as the advantage of being incredibly old. Almost predictably her skin begged for comparisons to aged leather in thickness and color, a splendid draping of canyons and folds and crinkles, a maze of lines that could be deciphered in a sarcastic variant on the palm reader. From this textured cloth peered her birdlike eyes, which maintained a magnificent lift as though carved with the swoop of a scythe. The heavy round eyelids must once have been swollen with youth but were now shrunken to the eyeballs and topped with crumbled, crenellated skin. She looked like an old cooked bird, he decided. A burned bird with sparse patches of dry gray hair in place of stray feathers. She would have looked dead were it not for the graceful motions of her almost beautiful clothes—confused layers of fabric, a breeze of pure color.

At the centerpiece of her small table was a glass of water, rather unspectacular except for its narrow proportions that gave it the appearance of an oversized chemist's beaker. Water was this medium's medium. She liked to tell the story of her life as though presenting her credentials, and she told it to Kurt: The day after her birth, her mother plunged her without remorse in a hole, chipping open the crust of ice sealing a small pond in Bavaria. Her mother saw the infant's eyes focus through the lens of water and knew she was a *chovihanis*—a seer, a witch. The icy water wanted to harden onto her newborn skin but she was yanked out, dried, and wrapped to her mother's breast. If she survived, she was strong. If she died, she was weak, too weak, needless to say. This test she passed and many others. As a child the water demon made love to her, possessing the form of an ugly uncle and raping her in a clear bath. He pushed her face below the water in his clumsy assault and through the transparent film she saw the black marks on the demon's soul. She knew then that she had been chosen. She was a seer, a witch—a *chovihanis.* Nearly a century later she has perfected the use of the thin volume of water that was her mystical, optical instrument, the liquid's thickness measured against the layer of icy water that separated her blind newborn eyes from the air above in her trial by water on the second day of her long life. And thus having explained to him the carefully measured volume, she examined the distortions of Kurt Gödel, his black goggles blurred, his body a thin filament reflected in the water. She then terrorized him by reading his fortune in the undulating image.

When she was done, the Gypsy crushed the glass tube. From the pool of water a vivid color bled into the Bohemian tapestry covering the foot-chewed floor, with its planks like splinters of eroded bone. The rug rushed with hues as though enduring a chemical color reaction until the stained cloth seemed to spill from the broken glass, a puddle a vibrant hue of blue. He did not wait for confirmation that this was a morbid premonition, a real misfortune.

He fell from the room into the rain that came from all directions. Defying the ordinarily uniform slant, it was a flurry of crosshatched streams that pixilated the scene and dissolved Gödel in the grainy solution. The Gypsy watched mute, endlessly surprised by the evening's events as Gödel was swept along the *Strasse*—a mere wisp, an apparition, a ghost.

When Adele arrived at his door, she found him waiting for her in the rain. His pale tincture convinced her to postpone her own report from the nightclub. Before she collected the coal, before she lit the furnaces, and before she cooked the soup, Adele guided him inside. There she listened with lips parted to reveal a waxy smear of lipstick on her top front teeth, as she kneaded the cold ache from his rain-drenched knuckles with her improbably hot hands.

His glasses beaded with water. Liquid pebbles refracted all images that struck his spectacles to create a melted kaleidoscope. Wanting to restore order to the world, he moved cautiously under Adele's patient attention. He tried to scoop his hair back into place with his one free hand to reproduce his usual thick, smooth dome but the waterlogged strands merged in wide flat bands and fell heavily, creating a deep part down one side.

"This world extends beyond this room, Adele. There are the

streets of Vienna and beyond that Europe and beyond that a globe in space in orbit around a star in a universe. But how do I know that for sure? I cannot see the globe spinning on its axis *right now* as I speak to you. How can I be sure? I can be sure because it's logical; the mathematics is sound and respected by the orbits of the planets. I can verify it's true, not by looking at it, but by *thinking* about it.

"I also cannot see ghosts, Adele. I cannot *see* them. But the Gypsy saw through the lens of water into me and past me and she saw them, Adele. I am not hallucinating. How do I distinguish a hallucination from reality? I know how. Unreal figments do not adhere to the principles of logic.

"That is *this* world. Figures of flesh and figures of air. It is unruly how they mingle and in fairness, Adele, in fairness, it is not always so easy to distinguish what is real from what is not. But beyond this world is another." With this his goggles steamed and his own eyes stormed with salty pebbles that beaded on his lashes. "There is another world of pure logic. There are no particles or grit or dirt or poison. There are perfect triangles, π, the number one, and it's impossible to confuse the real with the imagined. I get there through diligent introspection. I *know* this world, Adele. I know it through direct experience. I can go there any minute of any day by thinking. My mind touches it, this flawless reality incapable of deception." And then he wept openly, limply. A sad child. His spine a fine curve beginning on the wooden chair tracing around a deep bend until his hair fell toward the earth and tickled their clasped hands, sluggishly dripping water along the seam between their palms.

Lifting his head to her chest she cradled him. The angle of

his cheeks and the swell of his forehead against her body reminded her that he was just a boy really. As he sank into her, he said, "When I die, we must remember my soul will survive. Even if I find in my reincarnation that I am still in this muddle of partial truths and phantoms, I will at least be closer to that perfect reality. And when I die again and again, we must remember that eventually I will get there, to that pure, flawless place."

To help him feel better, Adele sang a tender lullaby, slightly off-key and off-tempo, like a pretty music box winding down.

DORSET, 1930

Lesions have festered in Chris's neck and chest. Tubercles rotting his lymph nodes, large nodules engorged by a calcified, cheesy pus near to bursting. When his fever gave way to chills and his insomnia gave way not to sleep but to delirium, he was rushed, by the master of his house, to a hospital in London. Surgery was performed to harvest the inflamed tissue. Not his first surgery, nor his last—that was to come within two days. The doctors couldn't know if it was the original tuberculosis, a fresh infection, or the compromised remains of overharvested tissue that killed him. But when the pain stopped along with his breath on the sixth day of his hospitalization there was no surprise, an irrepressible regret, and the faintest admission of relief.

In the two years since Alan had collected the broken glass from the blue solution that stained his floor, his anxiety distended and subsided in alternating currents. There were moments of utter desolation suddenly dispelled by joy. But overall the gloom grew, and he could not deny that in the middle of the night, possibly the very moment of Chris's decline, he watched the moon set over his friend's dormitory through the prism of his window. He wondered with unease if he would never see Chris's pretty face again. Alan's dread burst as gruesomely as Chris's infection when the statement of his death touched his ears. He was petrified with shock. He couldn't command his face or body to move. Frozen, he stared so deeply through the junior housemaster who brought the news, that the boy felt the very matter of his body invaded and struggled to stifle the urge to shove Alan away.

The funeral, to which he is not invited, is early Saturday morning, February 15, 1930. He kneels in the dark below his bare, fire-damaged windowsill and presses his forehead to the cold partition. His lashes tap at the glass as his nose fogs the window with two evaporating puddles. Alan tries to catch the stars that he can only barely see wobbling on the periphery of his vision, but they disappear when his pupils dart in their direction. Chris once grasped Alan's hand and dragged him away from their revisions in the library, dragged him out into the middle of the dark lawn to show him this elusive character of the faintest celestial objects.

In the weakening dark before dawn, the stars shine defiantly for a few minutes before the blanket of the rising sun's light snuffs them out. It is as if they are gone. But Alan knows they are still there, radiating in vain against the glowing yellow fireball on the horizon. It is an astronomical funeral procession. Chris is gone, but it is as if he is still here. Alan feels him radiating invisibly against the blaze of a new day.

VIENNA, 1931

Gödel feels stuck in this moment. Thursday. His hand on the door. He sees the blue of his own eyes attenuated in the glass. He is outside looking in at a man inside looking out. He takes in the taste of the coffee through the air and then the sounds and then the lights. He settles in a chair, near a booth, on the periphery of the Circle. Moritz creates a pinnacle at an otherwise round table. They are a ring of celestial bodies, rotating with respect to the distant stars. They orbit around an identifiable epicenter of truth, the epicenter seemingly near at hand, just there in front of each of them, but unreachably far away like a star in the infinitely far surface of the sky, like a star that they can almost resolve but then slips away.

Kurt wears his coat, the fur collar not as insulating as he would like. The cold aches through to his marrow. His lame heart is unable to sustain proper circulation, so that he is chilled from the vessels outward. The coffee warms his hands, but at the first sip his stomach convulsed with that habitual pain high in the back of his gut, slightly to the right. The rest of the dark brew sits untouched in its cup, an unhappy complement to the near overdose of laxatives he has managed to survive. He is appallingly thin despite Adele's bounteous production of food. "What, you don't like the potatoes?" she asks. "What, you don't like the stew? What, you don't like the meat?" He is driven to eat out of exasperation—to put an end to the interrogation over her cooking, and, of course, to make her feel good. Still, his combined weight, including clothes and glasses, is just over one hundred pounds. He keeps this secret beneath his overcoat.

Kurt has been silent for the twenty hours since his latest words (an inaudible good-bye) to Adele until his first words (a polite salutation) in the Circle tonight. His voice is surprisingly clear despite disuse when he interrupts the preliminaries of the discussion to address Moritz. "I have thought more about the Liar's Paradox, about the liar who says, *This statement is false.*"

Moritz appears not to hear as he continues to settle himself in and greet his friend Otto Neurath. Otto is a big man with big ideas and a big voice with which to spread them—a burly, charming, warm, but intimidating idealist. He came to Vienna after a short prison sentence in Berlin, a sentence imposed to make him think better of his continued agitation against the state. Otto pounces on Moritz's benign greeting, no doubt with his usual criticism of Wittgenstein, so that Moritz is holding his own ears, in mock annoyance, amused by Otto's persistence. Although Otto hadn't the patience to hold back his gibes, he did hear Kurt's attempt to penetrate their conversation. Still shaking his head so the brittle ends of his hair vibrate, Otto projects to no one in particular, "The liar says, *This is a lie.* The Cretan declares that all Cretans are liars."

"Half the lies they tell about me are true," Olga adds laughing. She takes Moritz's arm to find the table. Otto leans over to light her cigar and then adds cream to her coffee. She addresses Kurt without facing him while Otto fusses over her. "When I was a student, I was too impressed with those self-referential tangles. The Liar's Paradox, first. Then the barber who cuts the hair of anyone that doesn't cut his own hair. So who cuts his? The set that contains all sets that don't contain themselves, et cetera. These kinds of unsolvable problems are amusing, no doubt, but harmless really."

"Harmless if we recognize that they are utterly meaningless," Moritz adds. "Harmful if one is fool enough to get caught up in their loops."

Kurt nods amiably but says, "I do not agree."

"Ah, good, a fool," Otto booms.

Moritz leans back in his chair, his hair freshly clipped into a pristine edge above his ear and along the nape of his neck. He examines Kurt patiently. "The Liar's Paradox does not correspond to a fact about the world. It is meaningless. A misuse of language. Pure logic cannot possibly allow any such tricks. There are no unsolvable problems."

Kurt's thoughts touch upon several themes at once. When he is thinking most clearly he often sees things in big groups and not sequential steps. He can work backward and reconstruct a more linear formal logical argument, proving one step after the other for the purposes of a seminar or an article that is read from left to right one letter at a time staggered by a numbered list of equations. But this is not how the most beautiful ideas come to him. Sometimes they emerge whole without justification, like his theorem, which is not at all linear. It is self-referential, a tangled loop. A serpent swallowing its own tale. He wishes he could present his result to Moritz as it appears to him, that he could just open his mouth and have the fully formed shape stretch out. He tries to reassure Moritz, "I realize it is the great ambition," he stops and starts again, "But there are unsolvable mathematical problems. Facts among the numbers that can never be proven true or false."

Olga in particular is piqued. She first met Kurt through her brother, a mathematician and professor at the university. He advised Gödel in his studies and brought him into the fold. Her brother was fascinated by this nearly silent, intensely hard-working student whose potential for brilliance was evident. Olga was often asked to vet a student's work or to hear out an argument and search for flaws, so she was asked to listen to Kurt. She immediately took an interest in him although their first few meetings were odd—a blind woman and a silent man. Communication was minimal, to be certain, but whatever was said struck her as sharp and at times even stunning. Before long, Kurt spoke more spontaneously with her and a friendship was forged. Olga, better than any of the others, knows that it is Kurt's custom to speak extremely precisely or not at all. He is always quite literal in both his phrasing and his interpretation. So his uncharacteristic, somewhat imprecisely stated claim catches her attention. She has also learned to pay heed to anything he might say, no matter how odd a first impression it might leave. She has found that some of his deepest, most intriguing ideas create a complex sculptural image. Their value and meaning can be seen only with some effort. She feels for the metal tray with one hand and taps her ash into its bowl with the other while pressing for some clarification. "The Liar's Paradox is a consequence of wrongly used words. It isn't real."

Moritz interrupts with his hand stretched over his heart as though swearing allegiance, "There can be no such confusions in pure logic. What can be said will be said clearly. As Wittgenstein implores us, what we cannot speak of we must pass over in silence. *Tractatus 7,*" he repeats. *"What we cannot speak of we must pass over in silence."*

One of the new recruits, wearing—in the style of Wittgenstein that has spread among the younger members like a flu—a white shirt, no tie, knocks a fist on the table to concur as others rap on the wood of their chairs. Even Moritz is melting slightly from the inferno of Wittgenstein's ideas, although he maintains his own outward identity, and formal attire, proudly enough. He has caught himself attributing to Wittgenstein ideas that he is sure were really his own, thoughts he had formulated before that fateful meeting at Kundmanngasse. *"Tractatus 1,"* he quotes: *"The world is all that is the case. Tractatus 1.1, The world is the totality of facts."*

On every previous Thursday, Kurt has been a silent spectator. Tonight he looks from one person to another as he waits for the right opportunity. His temperature fluctuates while openings come and go until he throws out a question he knows they have asked themselves a thousand times. "How do you recognize a fact of the world?"

Moritz laughs, but not rudely, and nods, which loosens his

hair only marginally from its proper place before he stops himself, slightly sorry for his reaction as he takes in Kurt's serious expression. "It is a fair question," he confesses. "How do I verify a fact of the world?" Such a simple question. He cannot even answer this simple question. Despite his proclamations, Moritz knows something is wrong. No matter how disciplined he is in his adherence to logic, he cannot make sense of a method to verify facts of the world. He comes to ever narrowing definitions that magically take him farther from clarity. Spirals of rational thinking thread him closer to understanding only to unravel disappointingly far afield. As Moritz reaches for his coffee his motion is very slow, and it seems so even to him, the perspective telescopic. His fingers surround the cup and *feel* the heat. He pulls the cup to his face and *sees* the dark liquid. "How do I know this cup exists? I don't," he admits to himself. "I don't."

Being honest he can be sure only he *sees*. He can be sure only he *touches*. He watches Olga pull on a mammoth cigar. She has a calm about her, always at ease. The smoke drifts in curly plumes sifting through her lashes. She doesn't seem to mind and even tends to hold the burning cinder vertically and uncomfortably close to her eyes. Her hair is collected loosely at the nape of her neck, a rumpled frame for her big and broad broken eyes.

She cannot see the cigar. What does it mean for her to say there is a cigar between her fingers? The *meaning* of the statement is that she *feels* the tobacco-stuffed wrapping. She *tastes* the juice and smoke. She senses it. Does it exist? That is not a meaningful question.

But what really arrests Moritz, what keeps his fingers in a

frozen clutch around the cup, coffee suspended near his chin, is this question: Does *Olga* exist? He hangs there for what seems like a very long while. The conversation stalls, suspended along with the coffee.

"Olga?"

"Yes, Moritz. I'm here."

She reaches over and hooks his thumb with her forefinger. The rest of her fingers scramble over to clasp his hand. But all Moritz concedes is that he can feel what he has learned to describe as pressure on what he believes to be his hand.

Otto occupies the space to Gödel's right. He is doused in red—red beard, hair, and cheeks—a coloring that gives the impression that he is perpetually inflamed. He is a mountainous man of impressive physical stature. His beard grows in a dry and unruly tangle, a long web woven far out from his chin. The beard's natural red stain adds a fiery hue to his whole presence, a verve that he enjoys. He throws his weight around literally, but not metaphorically. He bangs his arms on the table for emphasis and backs up his resonant laugh with all his mass. In recognition of his formidable bearing, he draws an elephant to conclude his letters in lieu of his signature. The abundant fuel needed to energize his exaggerated bearing comes in part from deep moral and political convictions. He is literally heavy with principles as though the ideas themselves had been ingested and converted to the stuff of his body.

Otto's first wife, Anna Shapire, died giving birth to their son.

In his grief he would have consumed her if they had let him. He would have grabbed her by the handfuls and eaten her raw—muscle, fat, and bone. He would have refused to expel a morsel of her flesh. He would have hung on to her corporeal self, storing her in fat and glands forever. As it was he was restrained by brute force; it took several men and women to coax him down. So instead he gobbled up her ideals—her feminism, her social criticism, her visions of political change.

Her fluency in several languages he could not retain, and those languages passed through him undigested. But her vision of social and economic reform he absorbed intact and aligned solidly along his own so that he felt her initiative in his own decisions as he went on to positions of social and political influence.

His social ideals leave his large proportions restless, an agitation that occasionally manifests as a character flaw, one detraction from his generous portion of wit and charm. In those instances, he seems too keen to detect crimes of conscience and too quick to execute judgment.

Case in point: Otto harbors an unfading suspicion of Wittgenstein. He always probes a few lines of the *Tractatus* like a tongue in search of a sore tooth, such as *Tractatus 6.522: There are, indeed, things that cannot be put into words. They make themselves manifest. They are what is mystical.* Each time he says "mystical," he sings the word involuntarily and it hangs from his lips, an embarrassment, a blue joke, a crude limerick the others manage to ignore.

Another case in point: He finds Kurt odd. If it weren't for Olga, he might be more inclined to describe him as an associate, a stranger almost, than as a friend. Kurt's immunity to Otto's ebullient sense of humor is also a disappointment. In return, Otto finds Kurt's humor too clever and academic, so that the time one spends mulling over the setup and the punch line spoils a joke's timing, although Kurt often gets a genuine and spontaneous laugh from Olga. She has taken a shine to Kurt, as though he were a delicate bird with a broken wing but had the good fortune to fall into her garden. And he has impressed her deeply with his mathematical aptitude, so that it is more than pity he inspires. It is genuine admiration, and finally friendship, she feels toward him. Under Olga's instruction Otto listens to him more patiently than he might otherwise and has made a conscious decision to think over any of Kurt's comments carefully for subtleties of meaning.

He considers Kurt's question. He considers Moritz's response. How does Otto know what is real? He knows the ache in his knee from an old injury. He knows his son's arms and hands and face and growing legs. He occupies space and knocks into him as they walk together through the park. Otto knew an insidious grief that grew in spurts as childish and dramatic as the surges in his son's metabolism, but that has now abated to a sorrowful memory. And above all else he knows Olga. How does he know? He doesn't know how he knows, but this effete delicacy around reality irritates him. Is Olga real? She is Otto's whole reality. She is his love, his life. His guide.

Otto Neurath and Olga Hahn were married in 1912. He still describes to her the daily permutations of his parched beard, taking time to discuss the variety of reds that seem to alter with the seasons. When she fingers the coarse hair, she imagines ginger and rose-painted straw. She was amazed by the opulence of the most extreme sample of these dry colors, like the gold of Gustav Klimt's paintings. When she saw Klimt's portrait of one of the Wittgenstein sisters in 1904, lots of white and blue and green, she wondered where all the gold had gone from this wedding picture of an heiress to such a staggering fortune. By mere coincidence, it was not long after she viewed the portrait that she was blinded by a rare infection when she was just twenty-two. Less and less frequently she asks Otto to describe colors to her, the memories fading over the twenty dark years until she can barely conjure up a reproduction to match against his description. But she can always picture the blood and amber of his beard.

After she lost her sight, she tried to calculate in her head the way she used to calculate on paper, visualizing cool white marks like chalk on the bone surface of her cranium. But the initial equations would fade as the list became long and she found herself trying to work too quickly, a mad scientist racing against disappearing ink. After some years she abandoned her old methods along with some bitterness and found an aptitude she had discarded as a girl, reviving it accidentally when an unexpectedly vivid memory knocked it from dormancy.

She had an immaculate sense of direction. She and her girlfriends would clasp hands and whirl, the sun looking down on their counterclockwise orbits, their feet crossing and looping faster than they could coordinate until they'd fall over dizzy and disoriented. But at any moment Olga could close her eyes and point east with swinging arm cutting through the air's resistance, compensating for her stumbling. Even as she tottered on wobbling legs, with clear articulation of her index finger she could effortlessly point north.

She abandoned this spatial dexterity for a more analytic facility in her mathematical studies. Even blind, she still tried to record her ideas with pen and ink, knowing the mess she was making, quickly losing control of the page, and unsure of what wild assertion emerged from the residue.

Then it came back to her. On Boltzmanngasse 5 in Vienna's Ninth District, the sun on her cheek, a small mask of warmth in a sea of crisp air, the plain smell of the mathematics institute, and her arm a needle aligned with the earth's magnetic field.

Her teeth reflecting sunlight to the geographic North Pole. She found she could offer this skill in mathematical conversation, as useful as any compass when the others were lost. In the vast open space the darkness provided she saw turns and connections that the others missed. An aerial view of the hawk with night vision.

She uses her internal map of space to navigate in the solid darkness through rooms and streets; and her dexterity allows her some prettiness in her movements, so that she floats smoothly into the coffeehouse and glides into her chair, allowing Otto to light her cigar—a confident demonstration of her agility. Her spatial aptitude strikes her as a kind of biological magnetic phenomenon that she has learned to control and refine to the extent that, if she concentrated, she could map out her immediate terrain, her cup of coffee, the location of her companions, all with great accuracy.

Tonight she sits close to Otto, drawing on a fresh cigar, preoccupied with the juicy tang of the tobacco and the hot image of orange embers the burning cinder ignites in the memory of her eyes.

Moritz leans in toward her, his good friend, speaking conspiratorially over the ridge of his jacket. He leans near enough to inhale her smoke. "It's not that I think you are *not* real, Olga. You do seem to be here. I'll give you that."

"Well, Moritz, thanks for that."

"Nonetheless, it is meaningless for me to pose any assertion of your reality either way. It's not something that ought be said."

Olga winds the curly end of a loose strand of her hair as she listens to Otto snort (his nostrils have a flair for vibrato), her big elephant. He shifts in chunks about the balance of his delicate chair. His square and lumbering movements are a distracting, isolated earthquake. "The world falls apart as we sit at the table passing everything over in silence." He pulls at his beard to form forked fiery shapes from the wire as his volume rises. "What can we contribute as we sit here not saying things?"

Moritz is unperturbed by Otto's contentious mood. "In a sense the philosopher has no new truth to offer the scientist. But this isn't a disappointment. The scientific description is a world picture. Our contribution is to extract meaning from the astronomical and biological world picture."

Olga leans in. "Why isn't the scientific description enough? Here are the facts of the world: empirical discoveries. That list *is* the world. That *is* reality."

"Sure, one could argue the naturalist's case that the mind experiences an external reality in which it participates. But how can this account really satisfy us, Olga? One could equally well argue that all experience is highly subjective, that the only thing we really have is the image, the smell, the taste, and all of our assertions about the universe are constructions of the human mind."

Olga peels a stray feather of tobacco from her lips. "And this account satisfies you, strikes you as the truth?"

"It is rather that it is senseless to argue over which world picture is the correct interpretation. It makes no more sense than it does to say that the English description of Einstein's relativity is more correct than the German. The abstract structures are the same and in this sense both are correct."

"At some point don't we have to declare what we believe to be true?"

"Our propositions are true if they have the same structure as the world. Truth is a correspondence through structure."

Olga exhales, buying an extra second to find the phrase. "Moritz, are we really going to go so far as to say that we cannot lay claim to what is real?"

Gödel angles his neck forward to interject, "Numbers are real."

"I beg your pardon," Otto huffs with a pivot of his big shoulders, amused by his own slightly prissy phrasing.

Moritz's wire glasses swing the café lights around as if for effect before he enunciates, "Numbers are *not real.* They provide an abstract language that reflects the structure of the world, but they are not material, not real."

"Numbers *are* real. One, three, and π. I have empirical confirmation of the existence of numbers. I perform an experiment, such as imagining a perfect circle. I divide that circle by its own diameter to discover the number π. And you could reproduce the experiment. The mind's sensory experience of numbers is conclusive evidence of their reality. π is real."

"Real?" Olga offers this to him as a last opportunity to retract, or at the least to obscure.

"Yes, real. The most real."

With her elbow planted on the table and her fingers crooked to perch her cigar: "Kurt, whatever could that possibly mean, *the most real*?"

Many times before in their mathematical discussions, Olga

has felt his face vaguely with her blind eyes, uselessly skimming over his patch of space as though merely exercising the muscles. But this time she *looks* at him. She replaces her cup of tea flawlessly, anchors her elbow, and turns her profile sharply to pin the goggle lenses onto his blue eyes. There are principles, axioms, and precise rules for transforming them into physical possibilities. Olga violates those rules. Kurt considers the possibility that Olga isn't possible.

Kurt wants to tell her this world is not to be trusted. There are phantoms, slips in its rules. It is full of betrayal and deception, germs and poison. He wants to tell her that beyond this fugitive world is a better, truer reality, a Platonic reality, and our minds, through clear adherence to logic, are able to perceive that separate reality composed only of circles and lines, numbers and geometry. There is no disease, no voices, no deception—only truth. It is as though a lens of confusion intercepts all true lines and redirects the rays to a focal point beyond their vision.

Olga suggested helpfully, "Kurt, do you mean *real*? Or do you mean to say something about *truth*?" He considers confessing to her, "I know what is real only if I also know it is true." But he evades her question, although he does begin to speak to her with lovely clarity. He discusses the basis of logic and the form of mathematical proof. His frozen look melts; and the deeper into the language of logic he delves, the more generous he becomes—and feels. As Olga listens, she marvels at the unique cleverness of this man who was hard and sealed not but a second earlier, as though a match were struck to ignite his warmth and burn away the chill. He discusses the difference between proof and truth and narrates over the spare symbols that he has leaned to the table to draw but that she can't see. "There is a formal definition of proof within an axiomatic system but not of truth." Olga relaxes as Kurt resumes his usual formal, technical style. "One takes axioms through transformation rules to prove theorems. Truth is subtly different." As he continues, he knows he is offering her something precious, an incandescent gem, utterly sacred. He is offering something solid to a phantom.

The number 1 exists. It is real, even if Olga is not.

VIENNA, 1931

Kurt is running down Währingerstrasse. It is late evening and his glasses are slipping off the bridge of his nose as he runs with his head down. He overtakes a stocky woman carrying heavy brown bread and a bag of vegetables. He nearly knocks her over, his thin hip colliding with her doughy round one. He says he is sorry. His apology is too ardent. He is clumsy as he runs. He kicks his feet out to the side so that he trips nearly everyone he tries to pass. The sky is cobalt dark. The sidewalks are crowded with people returning from work. He makes it to the first corner. The Café Josephinum is only half a block behind him. He wants it to go away, to disappear. He turns to look. Otto is still standing squarely, holding open the door of the café, watching him run. Otto calls his name.

Tonight was the first time Kurt had taken the floor without invitation. His participation around the Circle is usually no more than a nod or a shrug, barely noticeable indications of complicity or skepticism. But tonight, over the glowing white moon of the table, across that astronomical distance, Kurt nearly whispered, "I have been thinking about the Liar's Paradox."

Moritz repeated with measured, deliberate timing, "Kurt, the Liar's Paradox is a misuse of language. In mathematics there are no unsolvable problems."

"But there are. There are some truths that can never be proven. And I can prove it."

Kurt wraps his arms across his chest as he tries to maintain his pace. The rain has started. Men are tucked behind the brims of their hats. They flow around him like the matter of the storm. Even out in the cold he can't shake the accusing blue of Moritz's eyes as he stared into Kurt's binoculars, damaging his optic nerve. "No," Moritz shook his head and folded his hands on the podium of his knees. "No," he said.

As Gödel crosses one street and then another he tries to strangle off his emotion. He feels nothing, a hose twisted dry. He is running away from what happened next, but his exchange with Moritz is in front of him, a recording replaying, enhancing with each circuit. Kurt felt the discussion take an ominous direction when Moritz gave in to the only impolite tendency any one of his friends might mention. He brushed his hair back with his fingers and lifted his eyebrows to share a smirk with his neighbors. It was only slightly demeaning but enough to burn color into Kurt's pallid cheeks. He tried not to panic. Trapped where he was in his seat between the others, Kurt offered to Olga what Moritz rejected. "The liar says, *This statement is false.* There is a mathematical equivalent, a statement that also makes an unsolvable claim about itself. It translates to, *This statement is unprovable.*"

He searched for the inky pen and wrote a spire of numbers on the table between the obstacles of saucers and cups as Olga read the tension in the stretching backs and elastic quiet. He outlined for her his numbering system.

"I encode the sentence, *This statement is unprovable,* into numbers—no words, just numbers."

"You translate the sentence into a numerical code?"

"Yes, a code of pure numbers."

Playing the part of the good big sister, Olga pitched forward in her seat, her eyes looking up as though waiting to receive a salve. She tried to catch up to Kurt's argument, keeping pace better than the others, still not quite there. "And then you prove the relation is true?"

"No, I prove that the truth or falsity of the relation cannot be decided by adhering to the rules of arithmetic."

"And so it has no mathematical proof."

"Exactly. But this is precisely what the relation asserts: *This statement is unprovable.*"

"So it is true?"

"Yes, it is true. We can recognize its truth plainly, not through mathematical rules, but from outside of mathematics. The truth of this statement does not follow from the inflexible chain of logical relations, the links that cleave one mathematical fact to another. It comes instead from a glance."

Otto could not help a certain amount of hopeful gratification with tonight's unexpected developments. Before they left their apartment this evening, Olga, cinched up in her high-collared white blouse, stood at the door bundling Otto into his overcoat, encouraging him to be civil. "Go and be civil, or stay and grumble," she advised even as she pulled his coat closed and knew he would opt for the go-and-grumble combination. His annoyance with Wittgenstein is contagious and has spread to a general irritability with all forms of authority, including Moritz's. She rested her face on the itchy fabric cloaking his big heart before holding his elbow and following as she pushed him out the door and they made their way to the Café Josephinum to spend an evening that culminated in this conversation as Otto said, "Are you saying Moritz is wrong?"

"Yes."

Otto drew a deep breath, making room for his belly to expand and then, like a Bavarian accordion, wheezed laughter into the parlor, slapping his stomach as he rose to order a cake from the bar. Otto was wholly entertained, elevated by adrenaline. The possibility gave him a start, an instinctive jolt. But Moritz took the news less well. Crossing his legs and arms as if to bar the very idea, coming as close to anger as Moritz ever gets, he tucked in his chin to point his words toward Kurt, the tone meant to highlight the ridiculous. "Is Wittgenstein wrong?"

Gödel's hands sprung out from within his overcoat, whittled down spikes ruefully warding off his own reply. "Yes."

There is nearly a roar from the students, but Otto applauded merrily. "What if Kurt is right? What is so bad?"

Moritz shook his finger vigorously. "It is cause for the greatest despair. *Reason. Must. Prevail.* And for that, mathematics must be perfect—and complete. It must be logically possible to answer all meaningful questions. It must be *possible*."

To which Kurt replied, "Mathematics *is* perfect. But it is not complete. To see some truths you must stand outside and look in."

"No," Moritz nearly bellowed. He followed with a back-handed swat at the air, holding his upper arm as though waving a flag. "No."

Reliving the conversation, deforming it slightly with each replay, Kurt turns left along the next street, then down two more. The wind kicks up paper garbage from the gutter. A piece of glass flashes from a tight wedge in a break in the pavement. The air is foggy around his mouth. A heavyset man is washing the windows of his unlit shop. The suds catch the brightest colors off the street before bubbling to a white foam. This man has washed these windows hundreds of times and will wash them a thousand more times, and a thousand more times they will be coated with a fine dirt. A couple argues quietly beneath a light from the window above so that they appear as though on stage on a corner they mistook for a private shelter. She is trying to understand his argument and he is trying to understand her bad temper. They are closer but they are not quite there. Never completely there.

Pelted by fat juicy drops of rain, Kurt is forced to accept that for all his preparations, tonight did not go well. He worried endlessly this morning that he might spook Moritz, that he might lose the respect of this solid, safe, sure man. He paced the floor of his frozen apartment until his ankle joints clicked and ached. But he had not properly prepared for this outcome. If he had been better prepared, he might not have made this grave mistake: He offered Moritz consolation, wrapped in a spiritualism that is repugnant to the man he finds so reassuring, so solid, so real. He should have stopped, but he couldn't stop, and so he went too far and exposed what he can't prove, what no one will ever accept, what will drive him mad, what is better off kept to himself.

His whole thin strand of a body pleaded, "Moritz," leaning in over the marble table and the liquid lines on its surface. His words were elongated into a lament, "We cannot prove it is true, but we can recognize that it is true. Our minds can see truth. See it even when mathematics cannot. Our minds are bigger than that. *Our minds are bigger.*

"I agree with you in this much: we can trust nothing, believe nothing, except logic and numbers. We don't know what's real. I do not know if you exist. You do not know if I exist. You may believe it to be true. But you will never know, Moritz. Never. All that we can ever be sure of is that 1+1=2. Our minds can touch it.

"Numbers are as real as the sun and the earth. They occupy a reality separate from this physical reality, but no less real for that. The mind is a gateway to this world, a gateway to another reality, a perfect place where everything else falls away. The world, Moritz, is not all that is the case."

In response, his friends who were collected around the small table, his colleagues, his associates, these strangers, very quietly continued to smoke and order from the bar and sort through private thoughts. Otto brushed cake crumbs from his whiskers while simultaneously pressing frosting into his mouth. The table was quiet enough that Kurt could hear the moist mashing of Otto's tongue against his upper palate. When every visible trace of sugar had disintegrated, Otto washed the gel sticking to his gums down his throat with a bath of coffee. The others sucked down the last of their drinks and then stared mute at the belly of their cups as if to divine their fortunes from the wet grinds. Moritz's gaze glanced off the table and struck no one in particular; his arms were still crossed. After a distinctly extended silence, Moritz inhaled strongly, pressed his lips together, and rested his interlaced hands on the edge of the table as if joining the proceedings for the first time. Then, unfolding a letter from a colleague in Göttingen, he carried the conversation delicately yet decisively in another direction, and the others seemed grateful to follow.

Choking on a shame he didn't fully understand, Kurt burst out of his chair, impressing Otto until he jostled Olga and barged through the room before fairly falling out of the café and onto the street.

He runs into the next district, turning left and brushing against the round back of a building until he is slung forward again, across another *Strasse.* These damp streets are empty except for the reflections in the puddles of people in bright windows in the flats above him. Kurt's foot splashes them away. They slop off to nothing only to reappear behind him when the ripples have settled.

A young girl looks out of a window and wonders who is down on the ground and how we got here and why. She admires the tops of the trees and a lone, clumsy man running and she thinks what so many others have discovered of themselves: We are not much. We are confused and brilliant and stupid, lost clumps of living ash.

I have tried to stay out of these stories but I am out here too. I am standing on a street in a city. On my way to a train. I see the girl up there in the window. She sees me out here. She is a thin invention of my own mind. Or I am an invention of hers. Or of yours.

Gödel sees her too, the girl in the window. Then she's gone. The window is empty. She has gone to run an errand she has run a hundred times or to wash dishes that will need to be washed again and again or to start a letter that will never express everything she hopes from it.

Gödel charges across the tram tracks, slick brass veins, skidding slightly, past periodically staggered trees and soiled curbs, through two more districts until he finds the place and bangs on the old sign. A bored man bearing a dense gray mustache leans into the gap made by the fractionally open door to say, "Show's over."

"Adele." Kurt wheezes, "Adele."

NEW YORK CITY

I have tried to stay out of these stories but I am out here too. I am standing on a street in a city. On my way to a train. I can see someone standing in a window several stories high in an ornate building overlooking the park. If I were up in that building, I'd look out of the window too and wonder who was down on the ground and how we got here and why and I would admit what I have already admitted a thousand times: We are not much. We are confused and brilliant and stupid, lost clumps of living ash.

On this street at this hour is an old woman in a huge old coat. I overtake her easily as she makes her way down the avenue. With the old fashioned streetlights and the backdrop of the park, it could be another decade altogether. She reminds me of Olga if she had grown so old, but Olga died in the Netherlands at the age of fifty-five after a kidney operation.

A woman and her dog walk toward me and move to pass on either side. She lowers the dog's leash so that I can easily step over and for a fraction of a second while my foot is suspended in the air, I'm a little girl about to skip rope and she's my friend swinging the jump rope handle. Then she and the dog are gone, along with the sensation.

In the park, over the low wall, there are two girls playing in the grass. Giants looming over their toys, monstrously out of proportion. They're holding hands and spinning, leaning farther and farther back until their fingers rope together, chubby flesh and bone enmeshed. What do I see? Angular momentum around their center. A principle of physics in their motion. A girlish memory of grass-stained knees.

I keep walking and recede from the girls' easy confidence in the world's mechanisms. I believe they exist, even if my knowledge of them can only be imperfect, a crude sketch of their billions of vibrating atoms. I believe this to be true. The girls are not a product of my imagination and I am not a product of yours. There are just some things that we can't strictly prove. So let's take it to be true, this is me.

I am on an orbit through the universe that crosses the paths of some girls, a teenager, a dog, an old woman. Maybe I should list more significant events that shaped my relationship to truth but that story would be a lie too. I could have written this book entirely differently, but then again maybe this book is the only way it could be, and these are the only choices I could have made. This is me, an unreal composite, maybe part liar, maybe not free.

CAMBRIDGE, ENGLAND. 1935

Seven years after the day that he is buried alive for nearly a full hour, Alan Turing lies in the grass of Grantchester Meadows. He came here by accident. He left his rooms in King's College in search of an apple in the open-air market in Cambridge's town center. The red apple skins in the first stall, usually his favorite, were papered with the withered remains of lettuce, evidence of an early morning transportation accident. After his initial revulsion, he considered buying the fruit and washing it clean but that option was dashed by the proximity of the red beets. The colors of the crops weren't exactly the same but they were in the same family. And some of the beets were touching some of the apples, which in turn touched other apples, forming a chain of spilled crimson contaminating the box and spoiling his appetite. He considered settling for a yellow or green specimen until he spotted a young bloke displaying scarcely any other produce except a crate of red apples balanced on a barrel.

He made a gentle approach to both the harvest and the boy but walked away with only the fruit.

It has been nearly six months since his boyfriend (former boyfriend) James left Cambridge, and Alan's loneliness has fostered a familiar melancholy. With his red apple in the pocket of his blue jacket, he lifted his collar, fastened his buttons, and found himself walking atop the old cobblestones of little Silver Street through the cattle gate onto Sheep's Green along Mill Pond and away from the slumping Mill Pub with its strong smell of beer in various stages of fermentation. Before long he was involuntarily committed to the pleasant hike to Grantchester Meadows.

He lies in the deepest of green pastures, quenched as they are by the special damp trapped atop Cambridgeshire. It is the early afternoon, although judging by light alone it might as well be evening. If he turns his head so the diffuse light collects on the stiff blades of waxy grass, big lumpy patches of the meadow look almost blue. High above him charred carbon is driven by the wind, like ash flicked from a cigarette until the ash resolves into a flock of little black birds. They swarm out of unison. Orchestrated but not melodic—the silent atonal drifts of unidentified black fowl and then they're gone.

Alan watches the birds flatly; a ghost imprint speckles his vision—white birds paling to nothing. An image of dust in his eyes. A phantom of shards of sea salt in a makeshift coffin.

Resisting despondency, he often runs here or along the river until it seems he might run all the way to London if he doesn't turn back within ten miles of the college. Sometimes he stays close to his rooms, if he has an experiment effervescing or a seminar to attend. And then he settles at the narrowest part of the river Cam, a roll of mud out of the opaque water merging into grass, a mere nozzle where the river nearly dies before it diverges, still within sight, to a proper flow, a body of water big enough to float the punts and rowers. Regardless of which spot he's destined to occupy, he is drawn outside into the damp and below the accumulation of clouds.

But the meadow is his favorite spot. He stretches out, deep in the grass and dirt, and imagines he is mud and vegetation, a bag of inanimate molecules reordered into a man. He is invisible in the grass from most angles and can almost see a full half sphere of sky from his favorite recess in the ground. More than once he has traumatized a hiker who strode upon him lying there looking into the stratum, and once he was struck by a bicycle.

He senses Chris's presence on these loneliest days. Propped on the windowsill of his college rooms is a cherished photo of Chris—a poor likeness, the unfocused image printed in reverse. The picture helps encourage Alan's fantasies and elicits his mourning more effectively than a thorn in his side, or a walk over hot coals. On receipt of the photo he writes a note to Chris's mother:

> My dear Mrs. Morcom,
>
> I was so pleased to receive the photo of Chris. It reminds us that Chris is in some way alive now. One is perhaps too inclined to think only of him alive at some future

time when we shall meet him again; but it is really so much more helpful to think of him as just separated from us for the present.

Alan has a moral obligation to achieve what Chris no longer can, because in some sense Chris is alive *now.* An individual doesn't just disintegrate with the breakdown of his brain matter. The spirit is a timeless essence. The soul's strength is precisely that it is not properly stitched to the past or to the future, but rather hangs there out of sequence and permeates time.

And so Alan feels Chris's challenge. He also feels somewhat less ridiculous attempting the imitation in his absence. There is no danger that anyone will detect the emulation as Alan's is a crude, misguided reproduction. This burden is somewhat lighter than when Chris was alive, and Chris Morcom's relentless successes contrasted harshly against Alan Turing's tepid failures. Although he did not live to take up the fellowship, Chris had earned the most prized of all scholarships, a place at Trinity College in Cambridge. Driven by his longing to be near Chris, and by his example, Alan struggled to drag himself up. Despite persistent failures, Alan finally obtained a fellowship to King's College in Cambridge, his choice second only to Trinity.

And here he has been ever since. Almost welcome. If not a complete insider, then at least not such an outcast. Even his sexuality has evolved without outright persecution. And he has a decent friend or two. But still he misses Chris and even spends occasional holidays with Mrs. Morcom instead of in Guildford with his own mother.

After Chris's death, Alan began a stilted exchange with Mrs.

Morcom to release some of his grief. It wasn't long before the stiff, polite letters buckled with emotion. He as much as confessed his love, using the word "attracted" more than she might have liked, but the implications were either ignored or sublimated. Mrs. Morcom was desperate in her own grief and sought any companions in sorrow, even this strange boy whom she could scarcely remember her son mentioning.

Alan justifies his attachment to the deceased since in a sense Chris still exists. To help formulate his defense he drafted an essay to Mrs. Morcom entitled "Nature of Spirit" in which he wrote:

> It used to be supposed in Science that if everything was known about the Universe at any particular moment then we can predict what it will be through all the future. . . . But this theory may break down as we study atoms. We have a will which is able to determine the action of the atoms probably in a small portion of the brain, or possibly all over it. . . . When the body dies the "mechanism" of the body, holding the spirit, is gone and the spirit finds a new body sooner or later, perhaps immediately.

Although Alan is agitated by his own faith—a faith that has never crystallized as well as he had hoped—he does not allow his spiritual leniency to corrupt his pure view of mathematics. As a tribute to Morcom, Turing analyzed sulfur dioxide and iodic acid in explicit mathematical detail. Beneath the differential equations and the chemical compositions he found a sharp result. Lucid and true. He recorded it in black ink on white paper. His proof did not glow in blue or throb with the thrill of the moment the beaker trapped Chris's radiance. But it was honest and right. His homage to Chris.

He writes to Chris in his diary, where he invents arguments about chemical models, or a blueprint for an automated machine, or a debate over K. Gödel's incompleteness theorems. He and Chris could have spent days together like this, talking all night, taking breaks with a game of chess. Alan is reassured by the memory of Chris shifting a rook back at Sherborne. Chris made a choice. He exercised free will. But still after all these years there remains a barb in Alan's head, a snare in his faith. Chris adhered to the rules. He executed a simple mechanical task. He applied some method. A computation.

Lying on his back in the lush grass with a view of gray sky, Alan thinks about choice. He thinks about rules. About method. About mechanization. He wonders if thought itself can be mechanized. The brain modeled by a mechanical process—by a machine. He wonders if a machine could think.

He draws the squares of a chessboard in a small, slightly damp notebook he keeps in his back pocket. Then he redraws the board as a strip, unfolding the blocks into a tape—the beginning of an infinite tape of squares. He draws 0s and 1s into the squares, crossing them out and starting again with small corrections. He encodes rules in the patterns of numbers. Then he draws a machine that reads the tape. He is not a fine draftsman so the machine is rubbed out several times and replaced with a simple illustration of a box. The finite states of his machine will respond to the pattern of 0s and 1s, will do as they instruct.

Before the late hours of night, still on his back, growing cold in the dew, he sees how chess might be mechanized because he sees exactly how to mechanize 1+1. He invents a machine that can add. A machine with no mind, no spirit, no soul.

His discovery shines in his thoughts. This jewel of his mind's systematic expedition casts piercing rays of gold through the rotating dome above him. Rising into the outright cold of the early night he stares faithfully at truth's gleam as he runs home, losing his apple, which falls from his pocket and gradually rots into the matter of the meadow.

But where is God in 1+1=2?

Each tessellated square of the small windows of Alan's room claims a different angle on the universe. He tries to select his favorite view. Sometimes it is the dense lawn of King's College. Sometimes he can trap a whole person crossing the grass in one square before the person wanders off, and then, as though the window is a fugitive camera, he tries to follow the image before it drifts beyond his frame. Today, and for the many days since his discovery in the meadow, his favorite view has been of pure air. He lies on the floor of his room, using crumpled trousers as a pillow, to contemplate the grainy canvas. He cannot bear to look at people. They destroy his concentration. So he leaves his room only for a run back to Grantchester or a run toward London along the River Cam. Occasionally he will stop in the town center for an apple and a glimpse of the merchant with the one crate of red spheres balanced on an old barrel. Then he runs down Silver Street, the sidewalk so narrow in places that he takes the uneven road the short stretch to the cattle gate. When he stops to close the fence behind him, he looks back in the direction of the town and marvels at how quickly his perception of the place is altering. His new worldview sweeps behind him and cleans away rubbishy confusion as fast as he can run so that what's left actually seems to glint.

As he runs through Sheep's Green, he avoids other eyes. The attention people require is disruptive. Once agitated, he finds it difficult to make his way back to the privacy of his mind. He runs through the fields until he feels he is completely alone. He catches his breath while leaning into straight arms balanced on bent knees. As he settles on the ground he thinks about numbers. About 1 and 3 and π. A machine could compute these numbers. The instructions would be simple and he could encode the instructions themselves into numbers.

Day after day he lies on the floor of his room staring into the piece of granulated air caught in the second tessellated square from the left and second from the top. Day after day he runs through the fields and he gets closer to the great idea.

He thinks of machines. Machines that follow rules written in code. His machines can add and divide and compute numbers, an infinite list of numbers. As he sorts the list of computable numbers in his mind, in his amazement, he longs to tell Chris, to catch him in the library or whisper to him during class, to sketch the numbers on paper for him, to show him the remarkable truth: There are real numbers that are not on the list. The list is infinite, but not infinite enough. He finds another infinite list of numbers—numbers that cannot be defined by any rule. A machine that tries to compute them will never halt. He finds an infinite list of mathematical facts that can never be proven. Uncomputable numbers forever beyond human reason.

He is uncomfortable and irritable, bloated with ideas. And something abrades him. His materialism escalates with these incredible epiphanies even as his awkward faith cloys and whines and nags him into misery. His materialism versus his faith. With a kind of morbid fascination, Alan stares at the brutal flaying of his beliefs with pity and a smudge of contempt for the loser. His own elaborate framework of spirit stacked on elements of matter, a frail house of cards that he easily blows apart.

The human mind can also be reduced to a machine. This idea drives all the others as he runs on grass, past trees, over bridges, through cattle. States of the mind can be replaced by states of the machine. Human thought can be broken down into simple rules, instructions a machine can follow. Thought can be mechanized. The connection isn't perfectly clear, but it is there, the catalyst of a great crystal. It is not just that thought *can* be mechanized. It *is* mechanized. The brain *is* a machine. A biological machine. The idea cools him from head to toe, a wave of understanding washing clean his confusion, his muddled notions, and his breath. Shock feels like this: There is no sky or earth. No time, no meaning. It's a throb—a hard silence, a pulse. It is colorless, tasteless, senseless. A white-hot explosion.

The wave crushes away his faith. He runs along the Cam, trampling familiar spots where he mourned Chris. His stride is smooth and easy and confident when the admission forms completely: *Where is God in 1+1=2? Nowhere.*

Over the coming days and weeks and on into months, he feels the last of his spiritualism evaporate like the cooling remains of a fever. He is left without remorse and wonders how he ever clung to his awkward faith with such emotion. We're just machines. At the age of twenty-three and for the rest of his life he embraces, without reservation, a mathematics that exists independently of us—although we, by contrast, do not live independently of it. We are biological machines. Nothing more. We have no souls, no spirit. But we are bound to mathematics and mathematics is flawless. This has to be true.

Where is God in 1+1=2? There is no God.

Looking back without the filter of faith, he comes to accept that the real meaning of his premonition all those years ago—a shattered glass beaker in a puddle of blue—the actual source of that foul dread, was not Chris's death, but the death of faith. It wasn't a premonition, a step over time's boundary or fate's dictates. It was an accusation, a finger pointing at his self-deception. Fear helped him deny it, choke down the nugget of realism, hide behind childish wishes for the remedy of fairy tales. But the discomfort lasted all these years until he finally let his defensive grip on spiritualism fall away. He did not mystically intuit that Chris was dying. He plainly witnessed his decline. He saw Chris's conspicuously gaunt neck and protruding clavicles. His poor appetite. His suppressed discomfort and probable pain. What Alan feared then, and what he now knows to be true, is that when Chris was gone, he was gone. When Chris died, so began the decline of Alan's faith. And when it was finally gone, it was gone.

To his great surprise his materialism is not so sad. He moves with greater ease and resilience and less fear. It is as though his eyes have suddenly come into focus from a nauseating blur and the whole world looks brilliant. All of his senses have sharpened so that colors and sounds and smells and textures are splendid and vibrant, his experience of them a heart-soaring joy. Every blade of grass glistens. The hard Cambridge wind batters respect out of him. The barren twist of every branch of every tree, even the weak fog of light, the whole of the world sings out to him as though he has never seen or heard anything before. With the sheer pleasure of this tactile awakening, his love of nature intensifies as though he has finally given over to her, wholly and without inhibition. Within days his spiritualism is no more than a mildly embarrassing, childish memory. In its place is a calm, impervious materialism—nothing like the sad, bleak emptiness he feared. He would have a bad time trying to put it into words. No single word could mean this thing. He would have to write something lengthy with many caveats and tangents and even then he knows he would not successfully express the immediacy or the splendor of the visceral experience. Maybe in another's mind better words would come, but not in his. And so his mind offers him something simple. Only one word comes to him over and again, and it could be only this—a word he doesn't often think to use: "beautiful." It is *beautiful.*

VIENNA, 1936

The worst year of Kurt's life. He has committed himself to a sanatorium. He isn't sure how he got here. Strictly speaking, Adele drove him the hundred miles outside Vienna in a borrowed car. He hunched through the front doors and with an imploring mask checked himself in. Before his signature was applied to paper, Adele was already only a forensic mark in the gravel, well on her way back to the city. That's how he got here. But the deeper reasons, the dominoes of cause and effect, they are difficult to disentangle.

There are determining factors in the story he tells himself to explain his trajectory. Without a story with its few key points, his life is a string of incomplete memories that he trusts even less for their accuracy than he did the actual experiences. From a handful of determining factors he draws inferences about his history. There is cause and there is effect. But then stories are distorted by inexactitude. He would need a clean and unambiguous calculation of forces and consequences, but the complexity of such a computation is beyond even him. If he cannot prove the answer, how can he know if he is free? Is he free to choose differently than he has in this moment? Is he free to choose to eat the crust of bread, or is the only choice he could possibly make this abstemious choice? He is not sure he can see the truth quite so plainly. In the absence of a perfect calculation he is forced to make approximations, to reduce down to just a few the nearly infinite forces acting to create this moment.

He has reduced the key factors to a list of five. First, he left for America. It took two attempts. With the initial attempt, he managed to depart Vienna on the Orient Express as Olga and Otto waved good-bye from one end of the platform without realizing Kurt's brother waved good-bye from the other. By the time the train pulled into the next station Kurt had taken his temperature several times and determined he was poorly. His brother was entirely disgusted to find Kurt had returned to Vienna dragging his luggage and requesting a doctor's attention. After a few days of coddling and convincing, Kurt and his train finally pulled away from a nearly empty platform, absent of waving friends and family. He made it to the coast of England, where he boarded a boat and watched the curve of land shrink into the fog. After he had spent six days trapped with brash American tourists, his mounting reservations over accepting a fellowship at the Institute for Advanced Study in Princeton, New Jersey, were dispelled by the sight of Manhattan climbing over the railings. His hope rose with those buildings. He was about to join, if only temporarily, a mass exodus of intellectuals from Europe to the New World. The refugees, from great icons to promising talents, settled in a pretty, wooded, and insulated Princeton protected by privilege and geography from the privations of an economic depression dehydrating the rest of the United States. Maybe in America he would find the recognition that eluded him in Europe.

He is still waiting for that recognition. He waits like a chronically ill patient requiring life-preserving medication. After his paper "On Formally Undecidable Propositions of Principia Mathematica and Related Systems" was published, he announced his results at a mathematical conference and was ignored by most, misunderstood by a handful, attacked by another handful. There was one man, a Professor von Neumann from Princeton, who pulled him aside after his seminar, and they talked as if their very lives depended on it. They talked about prime numbers and unique factorizations, coding statements about numbers into numbers; about proof; and even about truth. It wasn't long before an invitation came from the Institute for Advanced Study for a short-term fellowship in Princeton. After that terrible look of irritation and then finally grave disappointment from Moritz, Kurt's own disappointment had become an obstinate encumbrance. He never spoke to Moritz of his incompleteness theorems again and though they did speak from time to time things were never the same. It always hung about them. Shortly after his results solidified, Kurt's mood darkened and a short rest in an institution had been necessary. At least his mother and brother believed it necessary when they committed him for those few terrible months back in 1931. So when the invitation to Princeton arrived, feeling estranged in Europe, he accepted.

. . .

On his first day at the institute in Princeton he was greeted by at least one familiar face, the economist Oskar Morgenstern, whom Moritz had introduced to the Vienna Circle several years earlier. Oskar sought refuge in America after his brisk dismissal as the director of the Austrian Institute for Economic Research owing to what the Nazis characterized as his despicable politics. He established himself as an accomplished scholar at the Institute for Advanced Study and though grateful for the shelter provided by the New World, he often ached for the disease-rotted soul of his own country. On his first morning at the institute, Gödel entered the coffee room lined with journals and comfortably dressed scholars and there sat Oskar reading *The New York Times.* Oskar was anxious to hear news of his leprous home. "And how are things in Austria?" he asked, contorted with concern. "The coffee is wretched. What brings you to America, Herr Morgenstern?" was Kurt's astounding reply. When the conversation then turned to ghosts, Oskar was too flabbergasted to feel affronted and marveled instead at his new friend's "otherworldliness."

"It was so odd it was funny, so funny it was almost forgivable," he told his wife after he relayed the remarkable reply: "The coffee is wretched." While some of the other Europeans were offended by Kurt's airy, noncommittal attitude toward the Nazi troubles at home, Oskar did indeed forgive him and a friendship was forged. With at least one friend, some new ideas, and a general optimism about his future in America, Kurt was in very good spirits. Even before the new friend, the ideas, and his reasonable optimism, Kurt's spirits were high from that moment when he saw Manhattan loom over the railing of the boat. The good mood lasted until nearly an entire month had passed.

The second event in the falling dominoes of cause and effect that led him to sign the book at the entrance of the sanatorium was more nebulous. It developed during an otherwise entirely average colloquium held weekly at the institute. He sat in a typical wooden school chair that was bolted to the solid floor near the top of the steep narrow steps that led to the podium and the frame of green chalkboards. It looked like a yellow hill with wooden chairs in place of dry grass, with people tossed carelessly among the seats. Gödel took a place on the outside of an empty row. His thin legs, crossed in front of him, created a casual, angled barrier discouraging anyone from pushing into the empty stretch of seats alongside him.

He found these colloquia humiliating. Everyone laughed at the speaker's poor jokes. Everyone chatted foolishly before the formal opening remarks—chatted like old friends. They all seemed to be collaborating, working on the same problems, caught in the same flow, while he stagnated and watched them float merrily past. Young recruits to the institute advanced easily while he felt isolated, invisible. He wasn't generally given to bitterness, but the shiny ambitious world represented in the chirping conversations, the uniformity of seminar topics and speakers, the cohesiveness of the academic unit, magnified his isolation and his insecurity. Worst of all, the tacit agreement among the others—the team that naturally organized without him—amplified a feeling terribly close to failure so that his stomach acids bubbled and his bile churned. And just then he realized with deep despair and certainty that he would never quite fit in here.

His initial optimism on arriving in the New World only served to increase the height of his fall as isolation disoriented him. He was nothing, nobody, insignificant. A temporary scholar in America on a year-by-year stipend. No permanent position on offer. Not in Europe, not in Princeton. He forced himself to admit that the respect from his colleagues that he pretended not to need was not forthcoming. He cringed with embarrassment. He covered his hanging head with both hands to comfort himself for several minutes before straightening back into the room as if just remembering his current surroundings, the unbearable brightness of success gathered for the colloquium.

His walk home in the fresh Princeton air offered some respite from this restless sadness, but the relief was short-lived when he faced his single room and the shared toilet in his painfully lonely lodging. That night after the colloquium and the roomful of sweater-covered achievers, he lay prone in his bed and gave in to it, the third event in his approximation to his descending orbit, more decisive than the second—a swift and thorough depression. It was visceral and not at all abstract. He felt its onset more precisely than the unambiguous beginning of a head cold. First his metabolism ramped down. His blood pressure ebbed, his breathing slowed, and his muscles slackened. Down he slid into a desolation so arid he didn't have the enthusiasm to sob. But on the decline there were a few minutes of solidity when he felt just as he imagined other people must habitually feel. It was only a momentary pause during his descent, a rest allowing him a glimpse of the landscape before he passed by—not too bright, not too dramatic, but not hatefully bland either. Just crisp and clear and bearable. Then the undertow yanked him and he sank heavily in a viscous miasma, the pressure so imposing, he wondered why no one else could see the substance of his misery.

Over the coming weeks, even the few friends he had made were forced to stand safely back as depression tore through him like an overdue fire through a parched forest. Oskar in particular found himself helplessly throwing platitudes on Kurt's madness like feeble handfuls of water on a storm of flames. American doctors sent him back to Vienna with a nervous collapse imminent. *Get him home,* they advised. *Seal him in.* Let him speak German with a family that might hold him together before the dam breaks and the paranoia drowns him. He was only two months into his fellowship in Princeton, but there was no use protesting. He wasn't well. He needed to be home. He needed Adele. So he gave up his stipend, his rented room, and a last tentative hold on materiality.

Kurt departed on the *Champlain,* crossing the Atlantic on Friday to arrive in Le Havre within several days. From there he would travel to Paris before connecting to a train to Vienna—to his brother, to his mother, to his secret Adele. Oskar said aloud to the gaunt figure boarding the boat, "You'll be okay." But he knew this to be a lie and turned quickly to break his promise. He scrambled to send this telegram to Kurt's brother:

Dr. Gödel returns to Europe aboard the Champlain. *STOP. Suffering nervous condition. STOP. Fear the worst. STOP.*

As he dictated the telegram he emphasized each "STOP" wishing he could blurt the same command to the nervous wreck he had left on the dock. Stop. Stop. Stop. For Chrissake, stop.

The fourth event was the trip across the Atlantic, nothing short of a vivid horror, a black engulfing swirl that spat him up on shore, a deranged castaway broken from reality. No more needs to be reported of that sea-sickening voyage except that his brother left him in Paris, ignoring Oskar's telegram and Kurt's pleading phone calls. He hid in a small hotel of single rooms near the train station, terrified of the girl behind the desk, of her silhouette against the hanging keys, a frozen rainfall of brass. He wanted to die but the anatomical obsession with the preservation of his mortal flesh was an even deeper seduction—at least for a while. The delicate balance tipping in favor of life, but unstably. His suicide will be slow, excruciating, unimaginable. It will be the only possible outcome of these two drives finding equal strength: the ultimate impasse between the determination to live and the determination to die.

After three days of failed attempts, he managed to board a train to Vienna. Adele waited for him on the station platform, holding a handbag in front of her with two hands. "Come, Kurtele. I've made soup." Even though he was criminally dispirited, he coped for some months under Adele's care before the fifth and worst event. Moritz's murder.

The morning of his death, Moritz left his house later than usual, skipping backward out the door as he called good-bye to his wife. He was waylaid by a Wittgenstein crisis. Having chosen his words poorly in a heated discussion the previous evening, he almost alienated the man entirely and spent a good part of the middle of the night smoothing over the beginnings of a rift. Despite the loss of sleep, the late start, the missed breakfast, Moritz was grateful to be the one person Wittgenstein continued to address during his months of near total seclusion. Then there were days when he was unreachable, when his fury was hidden, along with his ideas. At those times, Moritz might spend their meetings staring nervously at his back while Wittgenstein faced the wall in one of the grand sitting rooms in his family's ornate mansion to recite poetry (mystical writings, no less, by the Indian poet Rabindranath Tagore). Moritz, an otherwise clever and confident man, was privately embarrassed by the obvious condition of missing some fundamental point. Wittgenstein once said, "You remind me of someone who is looking through a closed window and cannot explain to himself the strange movements of a passerby. He doesn't know what kind of storm is raging outside and that this person is perhaps only with great effort keeping himself on his feet."

Moritz was so enamored of Wittgenstein that he found himself traveling insanely across Vienna for any possible meeting with him as the philosopher changed venues at random without concern for the burdensome commute it might demand. Moritz often brought his assistant, a poorly paid scholar who kept his family housed in a two-room flat on Fruchtgasse above a Czech family of five in the crowded Jewish quarter on the wrong side of the Danube Canal, only to watch him be humiliated. Despite Wittgenstein's ascetic tendencies—such as living alone in a shack in Norway, teaching rural children grammar, shedding his family's obscene wealth in a myriad of ways—he still held an astringent contempt for Moritz's assistant and his abject poverty, a disgust he made no attempt to hide or soften. Wittgenstein's Jewish ancestors converted to Catholicism generations before, and twice he scoffed to an uncomfortable Moritz, "Does this Jew actually practice?"

Alone or with the decoy of his assistant, Moritz collected ideas like dew that condensed and dripped from the man's shirtsleeves, sometimes having the undignified task of mopping the dew off when it was reluctant to fall his way, so he felt, with disbelief, like a kind of manservant.

While Wittgenstein's frustration with Moritz and indeed the entire world often flared wildly, Moritz endured the rages and the fickle turns with characteristic patience. If any pressure was apparent, it was only in the form of an exaggerated show of this intrinsically great patience so that it was distorted in the direction of sycophancy. Moritz saw that Wittgenstein was not a madman, nor a bully. He was tormented, fragile even, sometimes crumpling like an eggshell. And so Moritz managed not to feel hurt by the increasingly frequent bites. Outwardly Moritz was as composed as ever and even seemed happy. And so it was on the day of his murder, he was composed and contented.

That morning, as he had for as many mornings as he could remember, he fastened his tie in an immaculate knot at the middle of his throat between starched collars, a tidy fold beneath broad lapels, layered in turn over a tailored waistcoat. Late for his final lecture of the term, Moritz crossed the *Strasse,* hurried through the grand university entrance, and cheerily skipped steps up to his lecture hall. In Moritz's quiet monotone, he spent many lectures on causality, infinity, free will. And though he may have been short of charisma in his oratory style, he was solid and informative and kind. He inspired loyalty from the full room—minus one. The one with the dead eyes. "He's not free," Moritz thought. He marveled at the futility of the week's preparations, the lecture plan like a casual stream of cigar smoke aimed foolishly into a gale. All events are set into motion, each causing others, until this event strikes as compulsory as the strike of a perfectly calibrated clock, the squeeze of the trigger predetermined.

During his brisk walk to class, he wondered about the role of quantum mechanics. At the end of the lecture, should he reopen the entire issue with reference to quantum randomness?

His argument against free will, a throttling of free will at the hands of determinism, was so tight, so clearly and convincingly executed. Should he unravel it so completely just at the end by pulling at the stray thread of quantum indeterminacy? Chance is a false hope anyway, a hollow distraction for the students to cling to, postponing their acceptance of the facts. Chance is not free will.

He bounded up the stairs, watching his own feet, still undecided and amazed at how it felt as though he were going to exercise choice. His black shoes held his eyes until another pair of feet eclipsed his view of the floor. As though engaged in a smooth continuous thought—the logical conclusion of his dilemma, the demonstration of the correctness of his arguments—his head rose to face the deranged lips, the untended hair, the white knuckles wedged painfully around the dark metal gun, to conclude, "He is not free."

At the top of the stairs he was unhappy to see his stalker blocking his path. A grim, gaunt, vicious boy with a schizophrenic's florid imagination. "I should not have let my bodyguard go," Moritz thought. When he had first come to learn of his demented student's jealous hallucination (involving Moritz in a torrid, and imaginary, tryst with a student named Sylvia) he tried reason, avuncular reassurance, guidance, and kindness. But for all his goodwill and earnest effort, the crooked ugly face of his assailant would not realign. The boy's steady mutation into a Nazi youth hardly allayed Moritz's own anxieties. The hair was cut so close above the boy's ears as to seem shaved in a full band around his head. The remainder was straight, parted on the side, and scooped over his head in a broad cylinder allowing a rope of black to hang over his forehead and balance at the corner of his right brow. His eyes seemed inordinately close together and he looked spiteful from under the dumb overhang of his eyelids. His was a pathetic imitation of the Führer, except the boy's hair was parted on the opposite side and wasn't tacked so tight to the head but lifted out of the suture, landing in a big round swell.

The wild, vitriolic phone calls disturbed Moritz's home night after night, the phone developing an ugly ring. Twice the rabid stalker had been forcibly committed to psychiatric wards. But then he'd be back, day after day nestled amid the human faces of boys and girls in Moritz's class, glaring like death itself with dead eyes, stupid dead eyes.

There was a gunshot to the heart. Two. Plus a bullet in his guts and one in his leg. The boy hung over him, blocking out the early morning light. "Take that, you damned bastard." He shot four times, tearing holes in Moritz's flesh. "Take that." At fifty-four, Moritz fell, crumpled and dead in a pretty pool of bright red blood. The look of shock and anticipation faded from his face as he descended and damaged his lifeless cheek on the stone floor.

As the blood poured from his tattered heart into the open air and his brain suffocated, all those incomplete thoughts of Wittgenstein decayed with the dying neurons. Neural connections in the gray matter storing memories and ideas in their ordered configurations fired across the gaps, last gasps of mental life. Thoughts on Truth and Will were erased as flesh sloshed soft and limp against alabaster, no more than rotting human fruit.

In his quiet room in the sanatorium with the narrow window

over the big groomed lawn, Gödel rested alone, slumped and motionless, and wondered, where did he go? Where is Moritz?

What does it mean to say that Moritz lived in the past? Nothing. The past does not exist. The notion of a past refers to a paltry and brittle memory, incomplete and flawed. Moritz is dead. He is lost but for fragments in the minds of those who have moved around the globe since his death. The Vienna Circle died with him as the headlines condemned Moritz Schlick as a Jew sympathizer who got what he deserved at the top of the stairs in the University of Vienna at the hands of a pan-Germanic hero who rightly killed this Jew philosopher. Moritz was a Protestant. Facts of the world are sealed in minds. People wear a facade. All of reality goes on behind their eyes, and there lie secret plans and hidden agendas. A tar of false motives and intentions. Truth mauled. Because the past does not exist except as a threadbare fragment in the weaker minds of the many. Moritz once framed a place and time in which things seemed more solid, more convincing. A place in which Kurt seems to remember belonging. Where is Moritz, who might—had they both been a little different—have been like a father to Kurt? Nowhere. He is not real.

VIENNA, 1938

A much-recovered Gödel waves a torn envelope across the table in which is folded a letter announcing the suspension of his teaching privileges on the basis of his previous association with Moritz and several Jewish scholars. This hardship irritated him into an actual conversation with Adele, using her as a forum for his complaint, which he expounded in legalistic detail. When he sealed his argument with a final conclusion that he knew was logically impeccable, an argument he hoped would persuade the authorities to reinstate his status at the university, he tapped his knuckles on his chair for good luck.

"Superstition brings bad luck," Adele warned.

It was statistically unlikely, he thought, but not impossible that Adele reinvented the phrase he has heard somewhere before. "Where did you hear that expression?"

"What are you talking about? I made it up."

Statistically unlikely, the thought repeated, but not impossible. Despite Adele's warning, he rapped the wood again and then unleashed the entire explanation afresh, incorporating every particular. When Adele was finally worn down with the revisited details of his rebuttal, he joins his friends at the café to wave the torn envelope across the table and fan scattered sugar into small dunes. Otto and Olga listen to the legal jargon with somewhat strained expressions.

As they take in familiar tastes through smoke and liquid, his friends already feel nostalgic for a home they know they have no choice but to leave. In vivid bursts, Otto describes for Kurt—and for Olga, who could only guess at the visual impression the massive crowd must have made—hundreds of thousands of people packed onto Heldenplatz last month to hear the Führer.

"He looked a bit effeminate the way he flopped his hand back to accept the salute." Otto narrates for his wife, still feeling the intense pressure of the crowd. "He looked ridiculous. His head bobbling around and those weird gestures with his hands splayed either side of his jiggling mustachioed face." Otto takes her hand with this feeble attempt to diminish the overwhelming ocean of Nazi splendor he witnessed.

"Olga, they wear red. Red against black. They have stolen our color. They have stolen our friends. Everyone is gone or going. Wittgenstein has left for England and his family has filed for a racial declassification. Under the new laws, they are considered Jews." And after a momentary almost embarrassed pause he adds, "We are going to be so lonely here that I am even forced to miss Wittgenstein."

. . .

Kurt enjoys the description of the monstrous exhibition but doesn't seem properly affected, as though Otto is describing an outlandish, impossible movie and not the fate of his own home. "They have revoked my teaching privileges. I am not Jewish, so technically they have no basis for taking action against me."

Olga cuts him off irritably. "Kurt, that is hardly the point."

And Otto cuts in too. "They *killed* Moritz, Kurt." He almost shouts, "Our Moritz."

Kurt will not relent, offering them further evidence from documents that defend his position even given the new social order pushing up around them. Otto slurps his caffeine in disgust and Olga turns away. They are quiet for a long few minutes when Kurt asks, "Olga, had Moritz forgiven me?"

After a full two drags on her cigar, Olga finds the patience to return to the conversation, and the curiosity to ask, "Forgiven you? I'm not sure what you mean."

"He never," but he doesn't know how to finish. He realigns his glasses. "He never said a word about my theorems."

"Ah, that." Olga's eyes seek him out but can't find him. Olga's image of Kurt is a quick drawing frozen at the age of twenty. Otto offered the description years ago, an impatient caricature. Big black round glasses. Thin. Very thin but with a round head. Round hair. He added the dark smudge under the eyes, behind the frames, as an unexpected but much appreciated detail. "Your incompleteness theorem was hard for him to accept. It was hard for all of us, for every mathematician alive.

But then Moritz always knew that it did not matter what he believed. What matters is the truth. And somehow you found it hidden where none of us could see. We all came to realize that mathematics is still flawless—no paradoxes, no contradictions—just some truths that cannot be proven. Not so bad. We can live with that. He could live with that."

"That was quite an event, Kurt. Moritz's expression . . . " Otto's generous smile is obscured behind the fist he snorts into. He tosses the fist away along with the mirth as he swats at the air. "Our poor Moritz. I enjoyed that evening immensely. Moritz needed a little conflict to shake him out of his Wittgenstein-induced reverie. But I have to confess, I thought you were wrong." He rubs his chest with his heavy hand as if that is where such memories are stored. "I really did think you were wrong."

"You did, didn't you?" Olga twists her cup in its saucer as she remembers. "I myself was worried from the start. Kurt, you worried us. It was hard for us for a time, to be sure. If not even arithmetic is complete, then what could we hope for from our philosophies, from our sciences, from the very things that were to be our salvation? The buoys that we clung to—perhaps, I would admit now, with too much desperation—were taken away." She leans against Otto and holds her burning cigar close to her chest. "And here we are again with our hopes being crushed. I used to believe that when I was older I would come to some kind of conclusion, some calming resolution, and then the restlessness would end. I would know something definitive and questions would fade. But that will never happen. Even now I accept that we are going to have to leave Vienna. My heart is thumping. My lungs are working. I am full of questions, changing this very second, affected by my own thoughts, never finished, never resolved.

"We wanted to construct complete worldviews, complete and consistent theories and philosophies, perfect solutions where everything could find its place. But we cannot. The girls I hear playing in the park when I walk to the institute, our neighbor the old woman who will die soon, our own circle, we all prize a resolution, a gratifying ending, completeness and unity, but we are surrounded by incompleteness.

"It was hard for us, what you proved. But you were right and Moritz accepted that. Kurt, Moritz admired you. He was proud of you."

With this thought Kurt stands abruptly to go. He says goodbye to his friends and though already half turned he adds, "I may emigrate to America."

"You too?" Otto calls after him, but Kurt doesn't answer.

Kurt meets Adele, as planned, on a park bench two streets away from the café. They look suspended in time while I watch them. Adele seems distracted by the girls in the park. Gödel is still as stone.

They leave the bench for the university so Kurt can submit his formal and finely reasoned response to his suspension. He stops her on each step to the entrance of the university to advance his argument. Mid-complaint, three young men attack him on his halting ascent up the steps. They wear brown shirts and ties with swastikas on their arms and leather straps across their chests that buckle onto leather belts. They look harnessed like dumb mules. Kurt screams to Adele. Is it his glasses? Do his glasses make him look Jewish? They kick and hit him until they can no longer bear Adele's merciless beating, wielding as she is a dangerous umbrella. One of the brownshirts is properly injured. After the assailants flee Adele's blows, she calms Kurt, pushes back his hair, and practically carries him home for repairs. There she washes him with fresh water and ointments, strokes his tender back, and hums to him to pacify his shredded nerves. "You see," she whispers, "superstition brings bad luck."

In a month's time, Kurt leaves Europe forever, traveling to the United States by boat, sailing around the globe, past Japan, past glorious California, to return to green and handsome Princeton, New Jersey. Something else is remarkable about that trip. This time he isn't traveling to America alone. This time he brings his defense—his new wife, Adele.

NEW YORK CITY

I approach a man and a woman on a park bench. His glasses, her handbag, her umbrella. They're as still as stone. They're in front of me and then, within a few strides, I pass the green-painted bench with its concrete feet. I turn to watch them but they are swept along by time, unable to stop, dragged away along with the street and the wind.

I see them everywhere, my two mad treasures. An elegant man in a hat with an able, stocky woman at his side. A solitary black-haired boy with a peculiar stride. I am looking on benches and streets, in logic and code. I am looking in the form of truth stripped to the bone. Truth that lives independently of us, that exists out there in the world. Hard and unsentimental. I am ready to accept truth no matter how alarming it turns out to be. Even if it proves incompleteness and the limits of human reason. Even if it proves we are not free.

They are here in our minds, Turing's luminescent gems,

Gödel's Platonic forms. There are no social hierarchies to scale. No racial barriers. Given to us along with our brains. Built into the structure of our thoughts—no bullying into blind faith, no threats of eternal damnation—just honesty, truth, and reason.

I am here in the middle of an unfinished story. I used to believe that one day I would come to some kind of conclusion, some calming resolution, and the restlessness would end. But that will never happen. Even now, I am moving toward a train. My heart is thumping. My lungs are working. There is a man, a woman, a bench, the glasses, the smooth hair, an umbrella. We are all caught in the stream of a complicated legacy—a proof of the limits of human reason, a proof of our boundlessness. A declaration that we were down here on this crowded, lonely planet, a declaration that we mattered, we living clumps of ash, that each of us was once somebody, that we strove for what we could never have, that we could admit as much. That was us—funny and lousy and great all at once.

CAMBRIDGE, 1939

Alan stayed in London last night in a small single room of a hotel with a window over St. James's Square after an afternoon spent at the headquarters of the Government Code and Cypher School, a division of the secret service. If he were allowed to tell anyone, such as his mother or his friends, no one would be more amazed than he is to find him engaged with His Majesty's government. His own mother considers him brilliant but perhaps somewhat useless. And he feels no more generosity toward conformists, such as he imagines members of the secret service to be, than they feel toward him. He once even joined the Anti-War Council. But when one of the Cambridge dons who had discreet dealings with certain military organizations during the Great War overheard Alan discussing a toy solution for the most general code and cipher (Who *didn't* hear that blaring stammer at high table?), Alan was brought to the attention of His Majesty's government. The work of deciphering enemy messages requires mathematicians, not soldiers, so Alan was recruited. He did consider declining the confidential invitation, but within a few minutes he knew he couldn't resist the promised puzzles. If there is going to be a war, Alan has to wonder what his part will be. The invitation, and his acceptance, forms the beginning of a somewhat unconsidered answer to this question.

He was surprised to see a classics fellow from King's at the training course. Given that the participants were expected to protect the secrecy surrounding the session, he felt implicated by the familiarity, as though he had already leaked sensitive information in the moment of mutual recognition. They left the course together already tainted by knowledge and forged a stronger bond of secrecy by taking wandering laps around St. James's Square late into the night as Alan kicked beads of fresh water off the stalks of grass. They talked while they moved as if afraid to stand still, as if pushing the whole earth around on its axis with their strong strides, as if afraid of the ecological consequences if they were to stop. They discussed nuclear fission and an unstable isotope of uranium. They discussed the potential for a chain reaction and the calculations that were involved. And when they were done they were too tired to discuss the implications and too tired to sleep. Each stood in the dim light of his own window after they retired to their separate rooms. If you had stood in St. James's Square at that moment and looked up at the hotel, it would have seemed as though they were standing nearly side by side.

They rode the train back to Cambridge together but in

silence. Without conferring they both opted to walk the long way back to college. As they skirted the edge of the town center, Alan spotted Ludwig Wittgenstein, Cambridge's most noted recent émigré and current professor of philosophy. Wittgenstein was stopped on the corner speaking to another man. They were both holding overcoats draped on their forearms. Alan thought he saw their hands touching. He couldn't hear what they were saying, but as he had missed Wittgenstein's class today, he didn't want to be seen. Grabbing the other fellow's coat sleeve, Alan dragged him down a narrow street to weave their way unnoticed to the protection of his college rooms, where he could begin an infinite experiment with the flip of a coin.

Wittgenstein insisted that Alan swear an oath to his class on "Foundations of Mathematics." Strictly speaking the oath was to the class and not to Wittgenstein himself although it felt like much the same thing. Alan made the pledge, as did the other fifteen attendees, but still he missed this morning's lecture.

"As Turing is absent, today's discussion will be somewhat parenthetical," Wittgenstein said when the minutes wore on and Alan's violation of his oath became apparent. Turing has become the focus of the philosopher's campaign to shake the idolatry for science out of people's eyes, so his course on mathematics has become a live debate between them. Alan is unaccustomed to philosophical methods of argumentation. The course that Alan teaches happens to have the same title but by contrast is a forceful lesson in mathematical methods, an impressive demonstration of logical manipulations of symbols, and nearly opposite Wittgenstein's in every way. Still, Alan does his best to defend mathematics in Wittgenstein's course while attempting to adhere to more philosophical forms of discourse.

The previous lecture he attended began as Alan's foot crossed the threshold (five minutes late) and Wittgenstein addressed him as if continuing a private discussion. He often treats people like books, flicking to a page and laying them aside until he chooses to consult a point on the paper. "Think of the case of the Liar," he said as Alan scooted through the seats. And the following dialogue between Alan and Wittgenstein ensued.

"Think of the case of the Liar," Wittgenstein said. "It is very queer in a way that this should have puzzled anyone—much more extraordinary than you might think: that this should be the thing to worry human beings. Why, the thing works like this: If a man says 'I am lying' we say that it follows that he is not lying, from which it follows that he is lying and so on. Well, so what? You can go on like that until you are black in the face. Why not? It doesn't matter.

"A man says, 'I am lying,' and I say, 'Therefore you are not, therefore you are, therefore you are not . . . '—what is wrong? Nothing. Except that it is of no use; it is just a useless language game, and why should anyone be excited?"

TURING: "What puzzles one is that one usually uses a contradiction as a criterion for having done something wrong. But in this case one cannot find anything done wrong."

WITTGENSTEIN: "Yes—and more: nothing has been done wrong. Where will the harm come?"

TURING: "The real harm will not come in unless there is an application, in which case a bridge may fall down or something of that sort."

WITTGENSTEIN: "Ah, now this idea of a bridge falling down if there is a contradiction is of immense importance. But I am too stupid to begin it now; so I will go into it next time."

In his ratty blue blazer and two different colored socks Alan rearranged himself to sit higher in the chair as he persisted. "One is most concerned that this should not happen in mathematics. But something like this does happen as Gödel demonstrated."

WITTGENSTEIN: "The question is: Why are people afraid of contradictions? It is easy to understand why they should be afraid of contradictions in orders, descriptions, et cetera, outside of mathematics. The question is: Why should they be afraid of contradictions inside mathematics? Turing says, 'Because something may go wrong with the application.' But nothing need go wrong. And if something does go wrong—if the bridge breaks down—then your mistake was of the kind of using a wrong natural law."

TURING: "Strictly speaking there are no *contradictions* in mathematics. It is rather that mathematics is incomplete. There are facts among the numbers that we can never decide are true or are false."

WITTGENSTEIN: "And so what? What could be the significance?"

TURING: "This means that not every well-posed problem has a solution. We can't know everything." He shrugged his shoulders as he looked around the class of pupils staring at him.

Wittgenstein did not pursue this direction. He did not explain how his opinions had changed (he had indeed pressed his thesis in the *Tractatus* that every well-posed problem *must* have a solution), or why they had changed, or even if they had changed. Instead there was a confusing digression after which he took up the argument again. "Maybe we are overly impressed with the Liar's Paradox, with Gödel's theorems, with Turing's uncomputable numbers, because we are confused about the *meaning of the words.* When you say the proposition is *true,* what do you really mean by the word 'true'? In what system? Is it sense?"

And so the debate wore on until it ended abruptly and rather ambiguously when Alan said, "I see your point," and Wittgenstein shouted, "I have no point!"

Wittgenstein stopped at the window, allowing an outrageous silence to accumulate. Finally he continued ardently, "There is no difference of opinion. Obviously the whole point is that I have no opinion." And then less intensely but no less mysteriously for Alan, "It can only be that we differ in our use of certain words."

Resolving a dark thread against the gray clouds, Wittgenstein's gaze locked onto one bird that broke formation. The bird stayed afloat long after the others touched down. Wittgenstein could see under the wings until the bird fell around a swell of air to show the black feathers of his back.

From his seat deeper into the classroom, Alan had a different angle on the bird, its left side, a flaw in the feathers, a beak in profile. As he studied the solitary flight of the bird, he saw the bird's purpose is to fly. Its brain executed a list of instructions and its wings and chest and feet coordinated their mechanical task. The bird collected light with its eyes, detected the wind with its feathers, spotted the rest of the flock or lost them. The bird is different from Alan only in degree. The bird is a machine. It has no soul. No spirit. But it has a purpose. The bird reminded him that neither he, nor Wittgenstein, nor any other person is so significant. This isn't a bitter sentiment. He can find purpose and pleasure and even meaning sometimes. When he does this, he is like the bird that finds the air and sings. He is every bit as significant as that bird.

In the irrevocable privacy of his own thoughts, Wittgenstein argued silently against Turing's admiration for mathematics, against his mechanistic outlook. He stood at the window in his leather jacket with his hair screwed up as though caught in a wind that penetrated the walls and glass. His feet were firmly planted to balance the tilt of his head as he tried to follow the path of the one lone bird while the sky filled with the rest of the flock. As a boy his heart raced at the sight of even the lowliest, shabbiest of birds. He tried to say their name, to give them a word, before his vocal and motor functions were actually able. It was a guttural thump, not the warble of a dove. Long after he acquired the familiar word *Vogel,* he still fought the urge to call out that guttural thump each time he watched a bird abandon him and his heavy sound, weighed as they were to the earth.

As a child, Wittgenstein longed to fly. It began with aeronautic ideas, then pure insatiable dreams of flight. As a young boy, the appeal of his handmade aerodynamic contraptions caused him physical strain. First they were no one thing, just wooden sticks and paper that he groomed into machine parts and assembled into a simple model, changing the design fractionally based on the few successful airborne moments of its predecessor followed by a weak flutter and a swift papery crash. He saw the initial skeleton so clearly, knew how to connive a lift from displaced air and how to ride the turbulence skimming the gardens of the Palais Wittgenstein. Sometimes he would pin the prototype to a delicate string, an ingenious kite, and pinch the end of the thread between thumb and finger while craning into the flow of the wind only to let go, his feet stubbornly gripping the earth. He watched his delicate structures come alive and escape the slight stickiness of his fingers. His favorites escaped the confines of the enormous manicured gardens, past the fountains and the blooms of primary colors, past the shrubbery and the walls defining the extensive grounds of his family's elaborate mansion. He watched his models with longing. His young brown eyes already handsome with brilliance—a beauty that would only deepen with age, enunciated by umber creases and thickening brows.

His specific acumen in engineering involved a methodical focusing of his general acumen in all matters physical. The external world presented itself to him as plainly as if he had been given a fully annotated schematic diagram of forces, actions, and reactions. This talent defined an aspect of Wittgenstein that so many admired. The intensely rational thinker. But there was a fracture in Wittgenstein's young life, a crisp break that split his life into two: Before and After. On the cusp of that fissure, too sharp and thin to assign a duration in time, blazed a white-hot light—only that's not right, it was the absence of light, but it wasn't dark. It was the complete absence of space and time and light and matter and it was closest to an eye-sizzling white, only these words were ineffectual, dishonest. They were lies. It had no color. It was closest to nothing he could describe in ordinary language. It was closest to nothing. Only it was a dazzling, shining nothing pregnant with ecstasy. It wasn't a thing; it was a happening, an event. The greatest event of all of his life. Only it was not parsed out in time and had no identifiable location in space. On the edge between Before and After, Wittgenstein flew. Not his body exactly. Not just his thoughts either. He—whoever, whatever he is—disengaged from the material of his flesh, from that moment, from that place, and experienced flight floated by the texture of that not-energy, that not-light, not-matter, not-white, not-dark. When he recovered himself, it was as though his body had been draped over him and the limbs reattached, superb prosthetics. Somewhere deep inside, only not in a place, but in a non-place he couldn't name, he was seared by rapture.

He never spoke of the event aloud, although he crumpled with a desire to frame it. Every word he tested failed. Nowhere in language could he find the sublime mystical truth that disfigured him. Then he realized. All attempts to describe his flight would fail. There were no words accurate enough. No pictures precise enough. All he could ever hope for was to frame its absence, a negative space carved out of the world. He could only describe what it was not. So he embarked on a complete description of everything in the world in a perfect logical language with the hope that in the negative space remaining, he could point silently to his treasure. The great architecture of the world and ordinary language would create a frame for the most precious of all—that which cannot be said. *What we cannot talk about we must pass over in silence.*

Wittgenstein stood with his back to the room for the

remaining long minutes of the class. The students sat in growing agitation as that afternoon was burned heavy minute after heavy minute like a fuel to power Wittgenstein's breath. Through the windowpanes he watched a swarm of students fly out of lecture halls and then form groups that crisscrossed the lawn. Their motions seemed organized at first, then disordered, then ordered again. Maybe class was over. It was time for the movie, he decided. He planned to sit in the front row of the cinema and allow the flickering lights to wash away the sweat and struggle of today's lecture. He turned from the window and took six big strides to exit through the heavily framed door.

That was the last lecture Alan attended, missing the seventh lecture owing to his training session at the Government Code and Cypher School. He resolves to attend the next lecture. Language is flawed but mathematics is perfect—this is what he will argue. He will try to convince Wittgenstein that mathematics is not a human invention, that it is there to be discovered, that it is the purest form of natural law. Mathematics has made us, not the other way around.

Wittgenstein hangs two overcoats on the pegs in his entrance. He decides to forgive Turing his absence today. He resolves to convince him that mathematics is an invention and not to be confused with natural law.

Each will fail to persuade the other.

Alan stopped attending the course altogether after the eighth lecture. When asked about Wittgenstein, Alan will explain Wittgenstein's comments and how he found them completely baffling. He will also say that he found him very peculiar.

Alan will not even try to articulate that moment in Grantchester Meadows when he discovered his machines, and Wittgenstein will not even attempt to articulate that moment in his childhood garden.

When Alan thinks back on Wittgenstein, one memory will always recur. He will remember having shared the sight of the black bird that broke from the flock to float on the other side of the window.

BUCKINGHAMSHIRE, ENGLAND. 1940

England is at war and Alan is in the middle of a reasonable happiness. We can pick up his story here on a night made unforgettable during a shave with a lethal blade as he faints from the sight of the blood. Of course he cuts himself—injures himself rather badly actually. Not with the razor, which cuts a clean thin slice tracing the bone of his square chin, but with the third tile, left of center, as he crumples to the floor and the hard ceramic connects with his hard skull. Just before the vertigo, he watches the blood slide down his jawline. The visual, along with the sensory recall of the feel of last night's dinner when his chin caught the chicken juice sluicing off his fork, mercifully knocks him unconscious before he is concussed by the floor.

For that brief moment before his mind goes dark but after he flinches from the sting and sees the deep red sap oozing into the cut, he calmly watches himself. The blood fills the split progressively like mercury climbing a thermometer. *I will next faint from the sight of my own blood,* he thinks, not as a statement of intention but as an observation of the unfaltering order of cause and effect. Push a key on a typewriter and a letter appears in ink on a page. The outcome is determined, a fixed consequence of the initial push of the key. His mind is no different. Press a lever and an outcome follows. Cut his chin, the sting, the blood flows, and he faints. He tries to hang on to this thought as his legs give way and his peripheral vision fades, closing down his eyes.

When he revives he is staring into the soles of his cast-aside shoes. Without hesitation, he reaches for them, sits up, laces them on his feet, and goes to collect the old baby carriage a neighbor has discarded.

As a wartime investment, he bought two bars of silver bullion at the price of 250 pounds. During the First World War, silver managed to rise in value even as everything else sank to a level of worthlessness that England finds hard to forget. While most investors place theirs in a bank, Alan has decided to place his in the ground. Tucking them into the dirty pram, he wheels the bounty into a nearby woods, drawing concerned looks from citizens who know better than to dismiss the sight of a messy young man with a peculiar stride and a lifeless pram. He prances like a horse, lifting the knees of his skinny legs hip-high and in a sharp motion. He prances especially when he is delivering a lecture in Cambridge or when alone with his thoughts, or when he pushes a pram heavy with silver bars.

It isn't only Mrs. Leigh who places a call to the local constables, living as she does closer than anyone to the woods and feeling, perhaps unreasonably, as though it is in her care if not actually her property. There is some confusion and embarrassment when the officers, ready for a proper interrogation, are told in no uncertain terms to leave the young man alone. There are rumors that these orders come from as high up as one could imagine—from the prime minister himself. Several of the local residents of Buckinghamshire already suspect something is going on at Bletchley Park, the mansion on the hill—something for His Majesty's Service or MI5.

Turing in his near total misunderstanding of ordinary human interactions thinks the pram *inconspicuous*—a *disguise.* A young father on a walk with his baby. The casual observer would never suspect that the little bundle is precious silver and that there would soon be a treasure buried in the woods. It hasn't occurred to him that they would suspect instead that a young father who entered the woods with a pram and left without it had buried something rather more precious.

One bar is buried in a shallow grave in the forest floor. He spends some time inscribing mental notes on the natural landmarks so no obvious human-made marker will be necessary. He takes note especially of the geometry between stream, grave, and a tree that seems unique with its branches forming a sequence of even bifurcations that he dwells on for some time, drawing them out as a graph and searching for a special sequence in the numerical relations—occasionally finding a rule sustained for at least a cluster of branches but failing to find one law that applies to the tree as a whole.

The second bar is buried under a footbridge, right in the stony bed of the stream. He encrypts the directions to the two silver bars in a code of his own design, rolls them into a Benzedrine inhaler, and slides the tube with instructions into a narrow gap in the foundation of the next bridge along.

As he wades through the mud in bare feet, his shoes and socks stored in the baby carriage, it doesn't exactly rain. That is, the water is not raining from clouds down to earth. The water is trapped in midair between mud and cloud, a kind of chilled steam if such a thing could exist. He is easily as wet as if the rain were coming down vertically. Droplets collect on his face and hair as he moves through the fog until cupfuls of rainwater bounce along his pores tracing the contours of his forehead, nose, and jaw. The raw cold irritates his fingers pink and his nose drips, but it might just be the chilled steam condensing heavily enough to produce a small grape at the tip. As Turing churns mud, tests markers, and invents rhymes, the gray of the overcast day saturates into an overcast night. He takes the balmy air into his mouth, sugared with syrup from the trees and rotting matter from the earth. Deep in his lungs the forest ether becomes his breath. He is made of the same molecules as the plants and the dirt and the air. He ingests them and they become him. He pushes out the air along with some spittle which soaks into the forest floor while his breath drifts and is caught on a wind that takes his vapors high into the clouds until he is just a small, solitary animal below and the hills roll all the way to London, fifty miles south, where the capital is shutting down, hiding in the dark, grateful for the fog.

He is just one particle in a vast system of billions of particles. He is connected to all the others through irrevocable crossings, points of contact, of cause and effect. He feels alone, but from this bird's-eye view high above and far away, and from history's view for that matter, he is part of some greater mechanism. Although he cannot tell from his proximity to the ground in the forest, from an atmospheric view that encompasses London, Oxford, and Cambridge, along with Alan Turing in the woods in Buckinghamshire, he is sewn tightly to the fate of the rest of the island. In turn, their fate is tied to his. And so Londoners (including more than one graduate of Sherborne School with a sorry bloom of ulcers seeded by a pit of dread) go about the burden of surviving, unaware that their lives depend on a young mathematician who digs in the mud even as the blackout is strictly enforced over the grand capital.

As Alan kneads sludge under the trees fifty miles away, air-raid wardens patrol the East End of London, trying to steer faithfully along the winding pavement and not to stumble in the dark with a twisted ankle or to fall atop a perpetually reinforced injury of the knee. They navigate by memory and intuition along turns and connections, past dead ends, along arcs and alleys covering the maze of streets in the hand-drawn map in their head to pound on the frames of windows, short and cockeyed old frames, outlined in bright shards of light shining through gaps in the blackout sheeting. The wardens, enjoying their cockney authority over the nights in the old city, pound and holler, "You've a light showing!" until the light inside is extinguished or the blackout curtain is irritably tacked back into place.

No one grows accustomed to the quiet just before the clouds evaporate one at a time across the sky as the Luftwaffe attacks. Molotov breadbaskets of thirty-six incendiary bombs burst open to spew thick trails of molten sparks and flame and a splatter of orange glitter. Some bombs thud lifelessly on cobblestone, like a flayed animal, still dangerously hot but quickly buried with a few shovelfuls of sand. Others stick in the crook of a rooftop or the join of two buildings or manage to penetrate a window, and these spread fire with vengeance, taking out entire blocks as the flammable sickness catches. Hardly anyone ever throws water on the small volcanic lumps anymore, not after the first few exploded upon being dowsed, projecting murderous lobs twenty feet in all directions. Tonight is more of the same. The sky lights up in orange flashes until swatches of the city shine with flames and London buckles and moans under the savage beating of the blitz.

Each night, Londoners grumble about the blackout; but by dawn they dread the sunlight even more, weak as it is through the filter of fog, as they are forced to take stock of the damage. Each day eyes sag with remorse, from the West End to the Thames, along east past St. Paul's Cathedral as the day tests their memory of their home. After fifty-seven nights of relentless bombardment each is forced to ask if his memory is up to the task.

In the darkness it is easier to recall the Roman wall around the old city in the east, the small cobbler's shop on the corner outside Blackfriars Station that labors in the shadow of the great dome of the cathedral and benefits from the cleansing draft off the river. The theaters that stencil the West End are still open and some gardens survive. Hundreds sleep in the underground stations or in public shelters in the basements of Felix and Lane's clothing firm where Mrs. Haddox runs a canteen serving beans and toast and starchy soups that manage to get eaten, even when shortages eliminate beef and flavor from the stock. Twelve hours from dusk until dawn pass in the stale air in cramped, unsanitary conditions, but still they resent the break of day when they emerge to have their memories confused by the scorch of earth where a redbrick Victorian had lived solid as stone just yesterday. Their eyes suck in a rash of hideous civic amputations until they water from the sting. As long as it stays dark, the whole of London might be intact—just as they remember it.

Fifty miles northwest, Alan Turing plays in the woods humming rhymes from the fairy tale "Snow White." Who is he to the air-raid wardens, the civilians, the survivors? A homosexual, a fag, an eccentric of the professor type. A heathen, an atheist, a queer. A genius. A hero. But they are no more aware of him than he is of them. For him, the war has become an obsessive game of searching meaningless strings of code for patterns, by eye at first on a lark and then through symbolic logic and the laws of numbers. He plays this game with bratty intensity, storming out of a room with a slam of the door if he loses. He wants to win. The work is consuming. It is challenging, maybe even impossible. There is something else worth emphasizing. It makes him happy.

He is always working, even here in the sweet-smelling dark of the woods. As he digs his hands in the earth shoveling away clumps of dirt he comes upon the root of a tree. A path through space. One possible path through earth. Then an idea fills him, presents itself to him, as if from nowhere. It is original, he thinks. And then he thinks about the thought. And then he thinks about thinking about the thought, about originality, about what it means that it's *his* thought. A product of his mind, a firing of a neuron, a picture in his eye, a fixed consequence of the push of a button. A reaction to mud. An algorithm executed by a machine.

There must be an algorithm for playing chess or for having an idea or for thinking itself. Press a button and a machine could execute the precise instruction and produce an answer or a move in a game of chess, or break a code. But then people all behave so differently. They respond so unexpectedly to the same input. Maybe someone else would dig here and have an entirely different thought. Maybe someone else would think, *Mud is filthy.* Or, *Tomatoes could be grown here.* He thinks about predilections, tendencies, and desires—how these are determined. He thinks about how he loathes boiled potatoes next to buttered rice. They are the same color but one comes in big lumps and the other horrid grains. The combination is enough to prompt Alan to fast. But his friend Joan loves her buttered rice topped with boiled potatoes. He and Joan execute different algorithms. They are different people with different tastes. Thinking about these thoughts he has another: There are many different algorithms that might produce some humanlike response. But surely there are many fewer right sequences than there are wrong sequences—sequences that could not produce a humanlike response. Maybe huge chunks of these wrong algorithms could be discarded somehow so that a smaller vein of correct sequences remain. But this is just like his original thought that precipitated the thought about thought. There is only one key to the encoded German transmission. It is nearly impossible to isolate. But huge possible combinations clearly lead nowhere; they are empty lumps of earth. If he could build a machine to run through possible combinations, a machine that stops when the combination goes wrong, then they could discard all of the bad keys, shovel them out of the way. They'd have a real chance of sifting through what's left, a far smaller number of possibilities. They shouldn't be trying to find the one right code; they should be trying to shovel away all the wrong ones.

The sky is caving in over London and he knows he has an answer. It burns his chest—a kind of elation. It scalds him.

As he starts home, he feels the Nazi code yield supple as silk and he can't wait until morning when he can implement his idea. Covered in mud—mud rubbed deep under his nails emphasizing the gnawed, red cuticle of each and every finger, evidence of the woods poking from his hair—he begins to run. He runs home freely without the pram or the burden of the silver bullion. His limbs are loose and lank, his wrists snap as his legs reach in alternating scissors, left, right, left, right and the skin of his lean body jostles slightly as he relaxes into the rhythm of his stride.

He will always remember running like this. Running with his lean strong limbs. Running as if the fate of the world depends on him.

Alan is engaged to be married. To a woman. She has been his best friend since he was drafted by the Government Code and Cypher School and this counts for something. He remembers her in Hut 8, bent over meaningless groups of letters, her neck tense and horizontal over the table hoping some pattern might stick in her eye. His clearest memory of her begins that morning after the woods when he wakes with his idea nearly fully formed—a Technicolor vision. He makes it to Hut 8 at noon with a gas mask strapped to his face and his sagging pants held up by a piece of string. And she says:

"Really, Alan, you are going to terrify the residents of Buckinghamshire riding your bike in here with that gas mask of yours."

"Keeps the pollen out, Joan."

"People will think we're designing poison bombs in here."

"But we're not. We're decrypting codes."

"Better that they should never think of what we're doing in here, Alan, than draw such attention to ourselves."

In the earliest days of Bletchley Park's conversion to the British center for code breakers, aerials to intercept German radio transmissions were planted in a thicket around the grounds so the mansion on the hill with its series of huts looked like an elaborate pincushion. Or, it had to be admitted, it looked like a center for code breaking. As this was counter to their secretive aims, the powers that be soon questioned their own judgment and the aerials were moved about the island to smaller, more inconspicuous intercept stations. All radio transmissions to and from the U-boats are encrypted on the German Naval Enigma machine, not much more than an elaborate typewriter. Press a key on the industrial-looking typewriter and the series of wired wheels and reflections rotates that letter to another on a bulb, which is then read and copied into the encrypted message. Enigma is capable of something like a hundred thousand billion billion possible combinations. It's a wonder that anyone has the audacity to approach a solution to the encryptions, which change daily. The coded naval transmissions are then relayed to Alan Turing's charge in Hut 8, where he oversees the dissection of the latest intercepts. They had the critical advantage at Bletchley of possessing a near-replica Enigma machine bought in Germany without conscious foresight for commercial use in a British bank in 1925 until that was replaced with an exact replica given to them by the Polish cryptanalysts. If they find the arrangement of rotors and reflections, they can type in the coded text and read off the German message.

The morning of Alan's nearly fully formed idea is Joan's double shift. She crosses out meaningless clots of letters and tries other combinations, making ample use of the flexibility of her thin white wrists and long, almost manly fingers. Her wrists are the size of dimes and from them sprout immense hands of bone and vein. At the base of these dimes are the stems of her arms where the constellation Orion was naturally tattooed in plain brown freckles. (The day Alan will break off the engagement, those limbs will hang from her like dry branches or maybe no more than sticks. Her huge hands pulling them down with dead weight. He will think her tiny wrists might break, and stare at them expectantly as he recites Oscar Wilde.)

Her hair is dark and wavy. He once asked one of the other cryptanalysts if Joan was pretty, being unable to decide for himself. The answer is irrelevant because Alan can never be sure. She has impeccable posture, her spine straight as an attentive child's, and she carries something deeply appealing in her mannerisms, a trace of the precocious girl still faintly visible. She isn't extremely graceful but she isn't clumsy either. She is efficient, even confident, as she maneuvers around the decryption machines.

She is glad to be here and enjoys her secret engagement to Alan. Although their engagement is rather more covert than his sexuality, this foolishly hasn't alarmed her. She is accepting and open-minded, a tolerance forced on her by her own position in society. Although the British civil service downgraded her title to "linguist," she was recruited for the exact reason that the other mathematicians were, for her cleverness and mathematical skill. She had been studying projective geometry and was quite sure her progress was more than promising when she came to the attention of the Government Code and Cypher School. It wasn't long before she found herself in the old Victorian mansion at Bletchley Park on the hill in Buckinghamshire, fifty miles northwest of London, earning rather poorer pay than the other mathematicians whose gender allowed them the title cryptanalyst. Alan and some of the others tried to arrange for her title to be changed to WRNS officer to enhance her pay. The ladies of the Women's Royal Naval Service tend the rotors of Alan's machines off-site, telephoning to Hut 8 when a machine concludes its task and the clattering switches fall quiet. But Joan, working in Hut 8, deciphering German naval transmissions, prefers the poorer pay in favor of the richer work.

Alan did mention to her his homosexual tendencies. She took the news easily, mostly because she wasn't completely sure she understood the term "tendency." She chose an eccentric genius and an eccentric genius chose her. It will not be easy to deal with his unkempt tendencies, his peculiar dietary tendencies, his obsessive tendencies—the homosexual ones are not her most serious worry. Of course, she is wrong about this. Alan should have been more forceful, even more frank than usual. He should have said, "I have absolutely no heterosexual tendencies," which would have clarified that his homosexuality is rather more absolute than his original word choice suggested.

Joan watches him the morning after he buried his treasure in the woods, and everything else seems far away, the smell of the London bombs, the creak and drone of the U-boats stifled by the ocean, the cricketing of machines. It all goes quiet, even the click of the keys of the Enigma machine. She likes his face most when it is as still as a photograph. The way his dark eyebrows accentuate his eyes does not look typically English and maybe this distracts people from noticing how handsome the accent can be, especially when he isn't moving or talking or laughing. She watches Alan unlock the tea mug he ludicrously keeps chained to a radiator, as though someone could possibly mistake the owner for someone other than Alan, as though any of the other cryptographers would put their lips to his personal cup, the inside walls horribly stained a rusty brown from the tea he always over-brews. As he kneels at the radiator to unlock his possession, his heels splay open and she sees where he tried to wash the mud from the bottom hem of his trousers instead of laundering the garment in its entirety. As she looks along his leg she can't help but marvel that even as he washed the cuffs, probably in the sink of his room this morning, he didn't notice the two leaves matted with gray mud into the seat of the trousers.

Alan and his schemes. In addition to the mug secured by steel links to the heating apparatus and his plan for the safe hiding of silver bullion, there is the government-issue gas mask he wears to defend himself against allergies. There is the alarm clock he tied to his waist to time his run from Bletchley nearly all the way to London. As well as the razor blades he wants to sell out of a suitcase if times get tough and he is unable to secure a job because he is unable to reveal the nature of his service to his country. There are his machines that mechanize thought and crack code. And she too, is she one of his schemes? To have a home and a wife to wash his clothes, bear his children, tend his house. He occasionally surprises her with these conventional social ideas, preserved relics of his family background. Maybe they survive despite all his other eccentricities because they are so utterly irrelevant to his actual life.

He brings the noise of the world crashing back upon her as he slaps his mangled fingers atop her papers, his cuticles bitten raw into a calloused scar, and scratches her pages of mathematics for a solution to last night's problem.

"Alan, you've cut yourself." The shaving cut on his chin is sealed with congealed blood, making it look worse.

"Yes. And I fainted," he hugs his torso as he laughs at himself.

He avoids her eyes, even as they share this minor calamity. Joan lets this disappointment touch her only for a second before she is equally swept up in the curiosity of the encryptions and the curiosity of Alan and she is laughing too, if more shyly, chin tucked into the cup of her shoulder, introducing a gentle curve to the string of beads that define her strong spine.

The ill-fated engagement isn't entirely Alan's fault.

Something is missing in his brain, a filter, an interpreter, a simple mechanism that explains the meaning of a smile or the current of feeling directing the hundreds of muscles in a face. Even the old woman who tends house at his residence in Bletchley Park seems a prophet on commonplace matters as she sweeps the walkway and makes wry comments as he comes and goes. "Your Miss Joan is looking for more than a chess game, Master Turing." Obvious, inane reflections of a meddling housekeeper but to Alan they are words of brilliance from a sage who knows things he cannot extract from life no matter how intently he focuses his attention. Exasperated with his genuine oblivion she says, "She wants to be your bride, Master Turing," and shakes her wiry shroud of hair as vigorously as she sweeps, with such punishing force it reminds Alan of how the Indian nannies used to scrub him red raw in the bath when his father was stationed on the subcontinent as a British civil servant.

All that day he was even clumsier at Hut 8 than he was all the days before. By the end of the afternoon after rotor settings were cleared, messages were collected, and cribs were tested, he and Joan were engaged to be married. You couldn't claim he had *asked* her to marry him exactly, not in any conventional sense. But still, by the time he retraced his steps to the boardinghouse and tracked chunky lumps of mud across dusted steps, he was engaged. So, in part, the engagement is the housekeeper's fault. It is Joan's fault too. But mostly, it has to be admitted, it is Alan's fault.

It is the end of an eleven-hour shift, the end of too many months of tense turns in tactics and encryptions and machines. It is the middle of the night. Alan and Joan are still awake but just exhausted enough for a game of chess.

"You're a hero, Alan."

He doesn't look up from the game, but his head sort of bobs about nearly level with his shoulders. He is embarrassed.

"We're all heroes, Joan," he says to her white queen, leaning too far over the board; the lower pocket of his open navy jacket slides two pawns out of their squares as he looks over the moves. He likes to get a nearly aerial view of the checked board and the static war they enact.

"If anything, I'm a heroine, you know," she says in imitation of a petulant adolescent. She glares at him with narrowed eyes, a bit disappointed that her sentence landed on an accusation.

"To me you'll always be a hero," Alan sniggers through his nose, not fully realizing the twist in the pinch he just delivered.

Joan takes some satisfaction in knowing she is going to win this game. She can already see it will take only two more moves that Alan is not likely to obstruct. He is looking for a global pattern again, trying to invent a rule for generating the right strategy so that he misses in particular this one reality, simple as it is. The board is hers, a worn cardboard pocket game not intended to weather the traffic of Alan's homemade pieces. It puckers upward in the middle when the pieces are initially aligned on opposing sides and then dips downward in the middle as the game advances. Alan must have looked quite a sight wearing a gas mask, digging in an exposed clay pit near Bletchley, and then attempting to balance as he cycled home with fistfuls of clay hanging over the rim of the steering wheel. He molded the pieces in his room and baked them on his own hob. He made extras, though not enough that they can play with an entirely undamaged set. One-third are broken to some extent but their identity is still pretty easy to ascertain, although one of her knights could double as a pawn.

Alan makes a move. Who knows what he is thinking? It looks random after all that deliberation. He still hangs over the board so that she has to reach under the fringe of his hair for her bishop as she shifts the piece into place with neither deliberation nor hesitation.

Amazed by what he perceives as her lack of considered thought over her strategy, Alan shouts, "Joan!" and cranes his neck to look up at her, though not square in the eyes. His mouth hangs open with disbelief and he looks down at the game and up at her a few times before shouting again, "Joan!" and then he chuckles, bewildered.

"I know what I'm doing," she says, and she does.

They might win this war. She catches herself fretting anxiously over what will happen then. There's hope and relief but also fear that Alan's scheme for her will fail, that she will be alone. She wants Alan to fret with her. "When the war ends, we'll be free. We'll have played some part in that."

While she may have in mind the freedom to finally marry, this is not where he is led through the labyrinth of his mind. So many images occurring to a person at once. So many different thoughts and different levels of awareness. So hard to communicate or to witness. The word "freedom" emerges in his mind, the final output after a chain reaction of impulses and transformations until it is there, the one surviving thought. His expression darkens but he pretends to concentrate on his war tactics, fidgeting with the dry broken pieces he molded with his own hands. Are these very figurines proof of his free will? "We're never free, Joan."

"Alan, are you contentious on purpose, just to be ridiculous?"

"We're not free. None of us. There's no such thing as free will. I don't know. I don't think so. If a machine can mechanically add a list of numbers, it is entirely determined and not at all exercising free will."

"But that's just a rote process; it shows no evidence of thought."

"Just because it's simple? Enigma is a machine; the outcome

of an encryption is completely determined by the configuration, more elaborate, but no more free."

"It's still not thought, Alan, not human, independent, free thought and action. Enigma is just a typewriter. I strike a key and it is entirely fixed which letter that key transforms into."

"Yes, it is entirely determined."

"Enigma is a machine, not a living, breathing person," like me, she is getting near to crying. *Like me.*

"We are machines too, Joan. Far more elaborate but that's all. One day there will be machines, like human computers, only electrical ones. A mechanical-electrical computer. I'm going to build one after the war, maybe taking something of our machines but I have a more general design in mind. It will add or divide or compute any number of tasks. It will be universal, like the universal machine that answers mathematical questions. Only this one will be real, not just a logical possibility." And grinning as if to himself he says simply, "I'm going to build a brain."

"It will be alive?" She accuses with the absurdity of the suggestion. *I am,* she wants to badger him now and her cheeks are prickling with resentment, *I'm alive, a human being, a free person.* In frustration she knows Alan will not recognize her venom.

"It will have electricity. I don't know. It's not alive? It's alive? What are you asking me, Joan, does it have a soul? There is no soul, no such thing."

Joan does not argue the point. She shares his devout atheism. Her father the minister could never get her to pretend. His sweet, brilliant daughter with the polite manner and strong presence, even as a very young girl. She listened to his sermons, sitting tall, the vertebrae poking above the white collar of her navy blue dress showing as little beads through her pale skin. His perceptive daughter, always asking "why" until he wished she were downright insolent and he could punish her. But she wasn't insolent, just convinced by the effectiveness of her own thinking, unable to believe in a God who wasn't rational. Unable to believe in God. She pitied him, wished she could lie, deceive him. She pitied her father as he mourned so heavily for the soul she didn't have. "The Nazis think humans are weak but their machines are invincible. But we beat their machines."

"But we are machines. Machines just beat other machines. One day the computers, they'll think just as we do. Will they be free? Or are they just determined machines carrying out the elaborate processes they are configured to execute? Are we free? Or are we just determined machines, bound to carry out the elaborate processes that each of us is configured to execute?" As if in illustration, he finally moves his pawn. He thinks he is just three moves from implementing his game plan. His weakness in this game, and in life, is that he is never prepared for how others will act. They are predetermined but too complex to solve or predict, and there are rules that he is just no good at applying.

"But none of our machines think. They don't make any actual decisions."

"Not yet, not yet. But we've just gotten started. It won't be necessary to build a different machine for each task. One universal machine will manage all tasks. It will be a matter of programming the universal machine to do different jobs. All these ten thousand people working at Bletchley writing down letters as they light up, mechanically changing the rotors, will be replaced by one machine. A mechanical change of the wheels will correspond instead to different instructions for the one electronic machine. And not just the mindless jobs but the jobs of the cryptanalysts too. Eventually the instructions themselves will be the domain of the machines. And then, Joan, then they will think."

"What do you mean 'think'? How can it think? How would you even know if a machine was thinking?"

"Ask it."

"Ask it?"

"Yes, if it can imitate conscious thinking, then who are we to say it is not doing so."

There is a pause as Joan internally tests her own atheism. "And if we are just executing programs, who did the programming?"

"Natural selection. Astronomical and chemical forces prodded the brain to mutate. We understand mathematics because we are created by forces that obey mathematics. That is why we can discover numbers and their relations, not because we perceive another reality—that's what Gödel thinks. But because it is part of our programming." And then he adds, "I am told Gödel is a little strange."

"Oh *he's* a little strange is he?"

"Yes. I almost met him once in Princeton a few years ago but he had a nervous breakdown and returned to Vienna during my year at the Institute for Advanced Study. Some of the logicians I hoped to meet then were absent but I don't think I minded very much missing any of them except Gödel."

Guileless. That's what he is, guileless. This stirs Joan's fondness as much as her resentment. "I guess he is just programmed to be strange. Like some others I know."

"Yes." Oblivious. Alan is guileless *and* oblivious.

"Alan, when you explained Gödel's incompleteness theorems to me, you said that there were true statements that could never be proven. Isn't that right? So Gödel proved that we can recognize true statements even if they can't be logically proven?"

"Yes."

"So if a machine is programmed to be perfectly logical, if it can only follow one logical step after another, how could it ever recognize one of these true but unprovable statements? And if it can't see a truth as plainly as you or I can because it blindly follows a series of instructions, then how can we call it intelligent? I guess I'm trying to ask if Gödel's theorems, and indeed your own, imply that machines can *never* think?"

Alan smiles uncontrollably as he nods rapidly and fidgets about on his knees. He loves Joan when she is like this. He really loves her in his way. "I would say that fair play must be given to the machine. It is not an infallible machine we want but an *intelligent* machine. If a machine is expected to be infallible, it cannot also be intelligent. Gödel's theorem implies almost exactly this. When we program a machine, we only want to get it started. What we really want, I suppose, is to build a machine that can adapt so that it is like any living thing that starts from a simple program and evolves a complex intelligence. Then we will have them—machines that are as alive as we are. As free or as not free as us."

He stops to chew on his fingers. "The machine must be allowed to have contact with human beings in order that it may adapt itself to their standards. The game of chess may perhaps be rather suitable for this purpose, as the moves of the opponent will automatically provide this contact."

"As your human opponent, Alan, I'm honored to be able to provide you with some proper standards." She loves him too when he is like this. She loves him, knotted hair, sticky complexion, filthy clothes, and all. Her own hair is not much better kept than Alan's at this late hour. It is frizzy and the curls have fallen loose but she knows he doesn't care any more than she does. "How could you write instructions that allow a machine to adapt? Maybe this won't be possible and it's exactly this ability of ours to adapt and change that makes us free."

"Yes, we change, but in a determined way. There is some input that is read by our internal configurations to produce an output that changes our internal configuration. So we change. This isn't freedom. We go from hating broccoli to liking broccoli. This isn't free will."

"What about creative leaps, leaps of intuition?"

"Neurons fire near other neurons, sending physical signals. The creative leap was inevitable, fixed in an internal configuration and the input received."

"What if someone could change your configuration? Give you a drug that changes how you feel."

"If my very construction were changed, then, yes, I would

have different desires, would make different choices. But then it wouldn't be *me. I* would be dead and gone. You are configured to be Joan Clarke. The choices you make are really just the output of a complex series of internal rotors. You feel free, but you are not. And neither am I."

Angrily, she grabs her knight, shifts the piece into position, snapping the top off the figurine with the force of her disconnect as she gloats, "Checkmate."

He smears his forehead in amazement and his mouth drags open as he scans the board for all the lost moves he imagined. Grinning, actually delighted, he comes to grips with this outcome, still perched high up on his knees. Then he drops onto his heels and says, "My hero. Come, Joan, let's knit. You can show me how to finish the gloves I've made."

WILMSLOW, ENGLAND. 1952

Here's what was missing from Hollymeade on January 23. An opened bottle of sherry, a clean shirt, a worn pair of trousers, unspectacular shoes, a reasonable set of razors, underused fishing knives, and a much-loved compass. Hollymeade is a semi-detached Victorian house in the middle-class town of Wilmslow, located a comfortable ten miles south of Manchester, where Alan Turing continues his postwar life with an appointment to oversee design of a massive computer at the University of Manchester.

On February 3, Alan went to the police station in person. He had discovered the name of the burglar, given to him by an informant. Meanwhile the informant waited on a bench across the street.

Arnold Murray. The informant. At nineteen his skin is already thin, his hair is thin, his convictions are thin. He is pale with pale eyes and pale hair as though color won't adhere, just as he won't adhere to anything. He can't maintain a job. He can't maintain a relationship with a woman. He can't maintain a relationship with a man. What he does maintain, unfortunately, is the expression of a boy who watched his mother get a beating from a father he never much liked. He once tried to escape by hitchhiking to London from the Manchester ghetto in which he continues to live with his battered mother and occasionally employed father. But he was swiftly returned to the cold and rain, unemployment and hopelessness of this same seemingly inescapable slum after a poorly executed theft resulted in a probationary sentence. Lacking better ideas, he drifts along Oxford Street in Manchester as he drifts through life, hoping to stick to something.

When Alan was at Cambridge, gossip used to circulate around Wittgenstein and the walks he would take along Oxford Street when he studied aeronautics at the University of Manchester. With its dark pubs and shops and anonymous pedestrians, Oxford Street provides corners and intersections at which to cruise for a bit of rough, maybe a poorly shaven young bloke. But really Wittgenstein's laps along the street were encouraged by fascination and terror at the occasional sight of a sensual boy prostitute. He never picked one up but he would race home to record his experiences and his desires in a childish code (in case anyone should steal a look over his notebooks). The exaggerations of Wittgenstein's prowess mythologized the sordid strip in Manchester so that from time to time Alan thought he would try a walk along Oxford Street himself with the hopes of meeting a poorly shaven young bloke. And so he did.

Having caught Alan's eye while pretending to admire a shop window, Arnold might have expected an invitation to the abandoned railway arches for a brief, illicit encounter but that was not among the short list of options Alan had considered. Instead Arnold was invited for a visit to Alan's home for a proper lunch, the table arranged handsomely with the help of Alan's housekeeper. Despite his chronic social tactlessness, Alan nonetheless had been born into upper-middle-class privilege and even adopted certain trappings of his class, randomly selecting modes, morals, and mannerisms and randomly rejecting others. His status and accomplishment made him better company than Arnold could have hoped for on the streets. This was the compensation for his crummy life that Arnold believed was at least his due. And so their affair began.

There were two dinners together. Some tea. Late evening talks on a throw rug in front of the fire. Some nights spent together. Though money did change hands (from Alan's to Arnold's), it was not, strictly speaking, prostitution.

Then there was money missing from Alan's wallet. Accusations. Some bickering. Some sulking. Apologies. A tentative reconciliation. And then Hollymeade was ransacked. While Arnold may not have robbed Alan of the sherry, the shirt, the trousers, the shoes, the razors, the knives, or the much-loved compass, it would not be unfair to conclude that the theft was in fact his fault. He did brag of their association to a friend over a third pint in a pub on Oxford Street—he had little else to boast about besides a liaison with a noted university scholar—and that rather poorly chosen associate from the pubs and the streets was the culprit who relieved Alan of this odd assortment of personal property. It would not be accurate to say that Arnold Murray was fully mortified by this beer-lubricated imprudence, but at least he was embarrassed and even sorry. As Alan passed the information on to the police at the local station, a contrite Arnold waited on a bench across the street. The next afternoon, two detectives—one big, Mr. Wills; and one small, Mr. Rimmer—rang the bell of Alan's door.

Mr. Wills had been an air-raid warden during the blitz. Each night he had patrolled Roman Road in the East End of London with its mesh of small side streets and dead ends. He'd bellow at the residents who carelessly left gaps around their windows through which lamps shone and illuminated the sidewalks, a small volume of light in the invisible city, a strict violation of the blackout. He'd rap on the window. "You've a light showing," he enjoyed shouting. There were several harrowing months before Wills's midnight patrols were abruptly rendered benign as the attacks stopped (in no small part owing to Alan's code breaking), although the detective's knee continues to ache from the recurrent injury sustained when he habitually misjudged the distance and fell off a curb in the darkest nights.

Mr. Rimmer, on the other hand, would likely have lost his life as a young slightly incompetent infantry soldier if the war hadn't ended with the invaluable information on Nazi transmissions that spewed from Alan's machines. Each of their lives feels like a solitary orbit through history, but these events branch off into a cascade of consequences like a web of lightning. This feels like their first point of contact with Alan but it is just one of many vertices. Alan in the woods. His idea. The breaking of the Enigma code. The end of the blitz. The winning of the war.

The assignment of an unspectacular case to a veteran detective. Just as Mr. Rimmer and Mr. Wills had unknown connections with Alan (as did a graduate from Sherborne School who spent some nights in Felix and Lane's shop eating Mrs. Maddox's soup), so too did the young man who burgled Alan's house. An officer just barely discharged from the navy, Harry the thief once served on a boat that was not destroyed by a U-boat but instead was diverted with the aid of the intercepts Alan had translated. There are innumerable other such connections and folds and twists of destiny that are too difficult to track and to compile in a list that would be too long to manage. So here we have only a fragment of Alan playing some part in his own demise.

Wills squeezes his formidable thighs into a chair in Alan's upstairs office, removing a spray of papers covered with calculations while patting the old wound in his knee.

"We are sorry to disturb you, Mr. Turing. We are sorry, but we need to clarify some aspects of your story. Could you describe again the informant who revealed the identity of the suspect?"

"He's about twenty-five years of age, five foot ten inches, with black hair."

"We have reason to believe your description is false. I rather thought that Mr. Murray was blond and not so tall as all that. Why are you lying?"

"Oh, dear. So you know of Mr. Murray."

"Yes indeed we do. And Mr. Murray is blond and not so tall as that. And rather younger."

"Yes, yes he is. He has thin blond hair, blue eyes. He's medium build and completely untrustworthy."

"Why did you misdirect us as to the identity of the informant?"

"Because we had an affair."

"An affair?"

"An affair."

"Would you care to tell us what kind of an affair you have had with him?"

"A homosexual affair. We performed three different sex acts in particular. Shall I tell you what they were?"

"Yes, all right, sir, why don't you."

And he does. Offering to transcribe the details in a written statement, five pages in a clear, official style that pleases the detectives' taste for technical language.

"It really is a lovely statement, like prose," the big one says, showing the little one, "although it is beyond me in some of its phraseology."

As they leave Hollymeade, Wills feels the littlest bit melancholy. "I'm only concerned about the professor's lack of shame."

"Yes," the little one says with raised eyebrows, and then solemnly, "me too."

"We shall have to charge him."

"Yes. Yes, we shall."

"Shame."

"Shame 'tis."

On February 27 Alan Turing and Arnold Murray are both arrested on the crime of Gross Indecency contrary to Section 11 of the Criminal Law Amendment Act 1885.

Alan hasn't seen Joan for years but even he understands he has to be the one to tell her. With anyone else—in the cafeteria at work, around the Manchester computer, at scientific meetings at the Royal Society—he talks freely, even loudly about the nature of the charges against him. His broadcast is an overcompensating challenge for anyone to dare judge him. But before the story makes the papers, as it will, he has to find more delicate, and hence less accessible, methods by which to tell his brother, his mother, and Joan. He wrote to his brother first. Alan's letter to his brother began, *I suppose you know I'm a homosexual.* That was all John read before smashing the letter into the pocket of his trousers, so he missed the close, which was, *When you come to Manchester, perhaps you will find the time to visit me in jail.* After his brother refused to inform their widowed mother, Alan took a train to Guildford to tell her—not explain, just state the facts. They fought, but not bitterly. What little she understood she cleaned off the surface of her thoughts and assumed a firm stance in defense of her most gifted (if undeniably not normal) boy against vague, unrepeatable charges.

And now he has the complex task of telling Joan. He drafts this letter:

Dear Joan,

I realize we have not corresponded in almost seven years so it might come as a bit of a shock to hear from me. Possibly an even greater shock to discover why. Do you remember when our engagement ended and I quoted Oscar Wilde:

Yet each man kills the thing he loves,
By each let this be heard,
Some do it with a bitter look,
Some with a flattering word,
The coward does it with a kiss,
The brave man with a sword!

And you said I had abominable timing both in my recitation of the poem and in my withdrawal from our relationship? Well I have gotten no better at poetry, I'm afraid, nor apparently at explaining myself. I wanted to be the one to tell you. I have been arrested and will soon go to trial. The circumstances are rather similar to those that permeated Wilde's infamous trial, although I hope they are rather less savage than they used to be. I told you I had homosexual tendencies. I should have told you that I do occasionally practice.

My home in Manchester was burgled. Everyone tells me I should have put the invasion out of my mind and let the incident pass, but it was just so wrong, Joan, and I couldn't tolerate it. I notified the police. In the course of their investigation it came to light that I had a relationship with one of the suspects. Well, he's not really a suspect (though I have my doubts). He's more of an informant. Intentionally or otherwise, as remains to be determined, he led the thief to my door. Well, there you have it. I was robbed and now I'm the one going to trial. I wanted to be the one to tell you.

My cryptanalytic days are soon over. I was assisting some cryptanalysts as a civilian but I'm sure you've heard the several inquiries that have advised the government to purge itself of homosexuals. They insist that the homosexual is somehow more vulnerable to blackmail or emotional and moral weakness. How they came to this conclusion escapes me. The weak moral fiber of those married officers engaged in torrid affairs comes to mind as a counterpoint. But you'd probably rather not hear about the rather grave consequences of my indiscretion.

He stops the letter, unhappy with the awkward tone he can't avoid. This demotion wounds him. He never boasted of his achievements during the war or after. Never spoke of Bletchley Park. Not to his brother. Not to his mother. Not to his few college friends. He never told suspenseful stories of the terrible days when British convoys were lost even while they held German transmissions in their hands, locked in an impenetrable code, when their brilliant ideas were set to work with ingenuity and speed and still what they got back was code and British soldiers died and they thought the Germans would invade and London smelled of ash and they lost night after night of sleep and hope and how it all turned around. These are stories Alan never told.

But he loved the work. The puzzle. The reality of the problem. The theoretical solution come alive as a material solution—a machine, a computer. And when it came to code breaking, Alan was a star. He was the best. He was even a leader, if an unorthodox one, in charge as he was of the transmissions that came in all day long from submarines, from commanders on land, from weather boats, from the Führer himself. He spent a lifetime in that brick hut with its hard floors that had grown veins and collected faint pools of water. The huts were crammed with wooden desks staggered in senseless arrangements and the desks were topped with a blanket of enlarged papers marked by rows and rows of encrypted text. Columns of WFLX and RTVN connected to columns of numbers and rules and guesses but still no German.

Alan could easily sift for recognizable plain text to use as cribs for thirty-six-hour stretches before succumbing finally to a previously unnoticed exhaustion. They all worked neurotically in a crowded room drowning in lists and punch cards and wire baskets loaded with incoming transmissions and empty of translated transmissions. The clicking of machine parts replaced the lilt of conversation as everyone leaned on the perforated sheets, pens hanging and drying in the air. They looked like students studying for exams from Cambridge or Oxford, as many of them in fact were. Women with hair curled into sculptured shapes wearing loose jumpers with rounded shoulders. Men out of uniform, professor types they were called by the Admiralty, their fingers buried in their hair and everywhere a blanket of sheets with scrambled letters that described invasion, the destruction of London, the Nazi designs. Their fingers touched these letters and still they didn't know what plans they described. Losses were mounting in the Atlantic, and England was choked off. Months and months and they still had nothing.

A person could attempt the hopeless game of arbitrarily setting the rotors and typing into the Enigma keyboard an intercepted encrypted message just to see what might light up. But there were trillions of possible wheel combinations so that accidentally finding the setting used by the German Naval Enigma was woefully unlikely. Then Alan had his idea from the woods. It was so brilliantly weird. They often knew a small piece of the plain meaning of any part of an encrypted message—the date; Happy Birthday, Führer; the weather. Alan saw how they could use this crib to rule out the bulk of wrong rotor settings, namely those that could not reproduce the small piece of plain text.

Alan designed an electromechanical machine that wired together a series of Enigma machines. He named it a Bombe after a Polish prototype. The Bombe spun through the multitude of rotor settings and pruned away huge bushels of wrong settings. This left them a fine tree of remaining possibilities to work through manually. There was some running back and forth to Hut 6 where Luftwaffe transmissions were sent. Everyone came forward to do what they could. Some of the other cryptanalysts came up with ingenious improvements on Alan's idea and he in turn made ingenious improvements on their improvements. A prototype was built and tested. And it has to be said, this made him happy.

His machines worked. Seven Bombes churning through the trillions of possibilities to decipher the transmissions. Churchill demanded the daily decrypts, sometimes a thousand a day, as many as he could get through, taking his favorites into the cabinet war rooms to inspire his tactical decisions. The prime minister even found the time to travel from London and stand in Hut 8, where he tried to clasp Alan's quivering hand. He had more luck locking onto Alan's palm than he did his gaze as Alan looked everywhere but in the face of the prime minister, laughing so anxiously it sounded like an alarm of yelps and hiccups.

Alan's engagement to Joan may not have been the primary source of his happiness. But she was his best friend. She stood next to him when he set the wheels and plugboard of the Enigma and stubbed his thumb into the keyboard to read off the letters as they lit up. She was there to ask him with uncontained excitement and pure anxiety, "Alan, what does it say? What does it say?"

"I don't know. I have no idea." She was there to take in his chaotic laughter, that machine-gun laugh of his as he stabbed his gnarled finger, "But it's German!" She was there for this happiness. And that counts for something.

Alan starts his letter to Joan again:

> Here's an amusing story I think you will quite enjoy. Almost a classic really. I went to Blackpool with some friends, my neighbors the Greenbaums. The wind off the ocean was terribly fierce and we had to lean forward so that everyone looked like they were frozen in a head-first dive into the sand. Along the promenade under the arches I spotted a sign for a fortune-teller, the Gypsy Queen! We stopped to get a rest from the gale and I took a minute to visit the Gypsy. As you well know I think psychics are complete rubbish but I still find myself drawn to the performance. It's like that beautiful animated film we saw together, *Snow White*. Of course I know it's not real, but still I love to see it over and over again. Remember how we couldn't keep our eyes off Snow White's every movement and we spent the

whole year chanting, *"Dip the apple in the brew, let the sleeping death seep through"?* Well the Gypsy Queen looked just like the Queen in *Snow White* when she was cast as a witch only even older, impossibly old. Her accent was so polluted I could hardly make out what she was saying. She put a glass of water in the center of this little round table and stared at me through the beverage for quite an uncomfortably long while. It was terrifying really. The reflection of her eyes was smeared around the glass into huge fish orbs. It was agitating how small the room was so that I felt there was nowhere else to look and in fact I began to get rather cross when she finally shrieked and knocked the table over, smashing the glass. I don't know what she was calling out but it was shrill and raised the hairs on my neck. I shrieked too and fled. I was thoroughly rattled and rather made a fool of myself. I fell out from under the purple drapery she had hanging in the doorway, white as a ghost according to my friends, and ran down the beach into a rainstorm so thick I thought I would dissolve! My friends found me at the bus stop and we traveled back to Manchester together but I was unable to utter a single word. I felt a complete buffoon, naturally. My neighbors haven't yet returned my call and I wonder if they ever will. The incident matched the time I woke everyone at Bletchley in the middle of the night because I thought I had accidentally poisoned myself. Remember, you had to convince the security officers that I wasn't a National Hazard? I wish you were here to convince the Greenbaums.

Work on the Manchester computer moves forward and I feel certain that these machines will be indispensable one day and that the machines will even think so themselves! At least you would find it more challenging to beat one at chess than it was to beat me.

Congratulations on your recent engagement.

Sincerest regards,
Alan Turing

Alan tears up his letter to Joan and sends this instead:

February 4, 1952

Dear Joan,

I wanted to be the one to tell you that I have been arrested for Gross Indecency contrary to Section 11 of the Criminal Law Amendment Act 1885. There will be a trial and you should be prepared to read of the unpleasantness in the paper. During the war I told you of my homosexual tendencies. I should have told you that I do occasionally practice. I can only hope that they are rather less savage than they were in Oscar Wilde's day.

The whole saga rather outstrips the time I was momentarily arrested upon emerging from the woods after depositing my silver bullion in the stream. As I recall, you were rather delighted by that episode. If I am not incarcerated, I must go back to Buckinghamshire one of these days and recover my investment.

I do remember those times, and our friendship, rather fondly.

Best wishes on your recent engagement.

Sincerest regards,
A. M. Turing

PRINCETON, AMERICA. 1977

On the edge of Princeton in a simple, low, rectangular house Kurt eats a single egg for breakfast and a teaspoon of tea. The day begins well with a nearly perfect bowel movement. Then Adele prepares his breakfast without incident and seems less persistent than usual in her attempts to spoon-feed him more food than his habitual single egg and teaspoon of tea. He has perfectly tuned his intake of specific foods, balanced precisely against his intake of Milk of Magnesia and ExLax—balanced to the drop. This has controlled his ulcer, which hemorrhaged last year, and ameliorated the associated stomach pain, high up and to the right, deep in the back, so high and deep it almost burns the atrium of his heart through the linings of his organs. The carefully timed administration of morsel of food versus laxative has also tamed both his indigestion and his constipation. It has taken him two decades to work out the schedule so precisely. The diary he maintains of his daily gastrointestinal cycle, his temperature, and his bowel movements has been invaluable in working out his own prescription.

After breakfast, he isolates himself at his spare desk. He barely goes to the institute anymore. The advantage is privacy. The disadvantage is the proximity of Adele's unmodulated attention. But today she does not resist his escape to his desk. She is almost subdued and he hardly even notices her milling about, tidying up. He doesn't know what he will work on today. His ideas have been fractured, unfocused. He hasn't found the ambition he needs to complete a calculation or a paper in so long he worries it might actually be years.

Adele is finished with this room, but she likes to be near Kurt, so she bends over, making a wide, low shape and begins to wipe the faint hint of dust from the baseboards near his desk. Over her shoulder, she begins a mild complaint about the housekeeper, a strong Pole whom she gratefully befriended, but for reasons even Adele can't fathom the weak tirade peters off. It is almost as though she doesn't feel like talking today. She just feels like being near.

"There is almost no one left to talk to," he tells Adele, speaking toward her haunches.

Kurt is in a strange mood today too. "So, talk to me," she says. Her arms feel heavy, wobbly.

"If Einstein were here, I might still go to the institute."

"Yes," she says, finding renewed purpose behind her task. "But he's been gone twenty years. You still have Oskar," Adele says. "Be grateful."

He is grateful. Kurt sends Adele out of the house so he can

phone his last living friend, Oskar Morgenstern. "Adele-la, would you bring me an apple from the store?"

"Yes, Kurtele. Sure. Why not? An apple." She pulls herself up, wipes her hands with the nearly clean back side of the rag and pets Kurt's head just once as she leaves the room, collects her coat from a peg in the hall, and closes the latch on the door behind her.

Kurt dials the number he remembers better than his own.

"Hello," Oskar answers.

"No one at the institute respects me."

Wanting to spare his wife the taxing repetition that Kurt's phone calls demand, Oskar mouths silently to his wife, "Gödel," and waves her away. "Kurt, *I* respect you."

"It was *twenty years* before I was made professor." His voice is strained.

"Yes, Kurt. This was wrong," Oskar concedes genuinely. "This was wrong."

"If I die, you must promise to publish my article refuting Alan Turing's thesis on the limits of the mind. A Turing machine is a concept, equivalent to a mechanical procedure or algorithm. Turing was able to completely replace reasoning by mechanical operations on formulas—by Turing machines. Good, agreed? However, are we supposed to equate the human soul with a Turing machine? No. There is a philosophical error in Turing's work. Turing in his 1937 paper, page 250, gives an argument which is supposed to show that mental procedures cannot go beyond mechanical procedures. However this argument is inconclusive. What Turing disregards completely is the fact that mind, in its use, is not static, but constantly developing. They murdered him, you realize?"

"I thought it was suicide," Oskar replies absently.

Kurt continues, "The government poisoned his food. I have also been working on a formal proof of the existence of God. But this is still unfinished. I don't want our colleagues to think I am crazy. Maybe you should not publish that one if I die."

"Kurt, *I'm* the one who's dying!" Oskar entreats.

Gödel dismisses Oskar's illness. "Your legs will soon recover from paralysis," Kurt says, pulled rapidly back to the indulgence of his own mire.

"Kurt, I have cancer. Cancer! I will not get better."

"The cancer will recede."

"No, Kurt, no it will not. It has metastasized. It will not recede. I cannot negotiate with your publishers anymore. Nor with your doctors. Nor with your wife," who, to be honest, Oskar never liked. He found Adele vulgar, and Kurt's attraction to her was an annoying mystery. He complained to his own wife, "She's a Viennese washerwoman type: garrulous, uncultured, strong-willed." When Adele laughed her dirty teeth showed. Oskar always awaited a snort or two though, to be fair, they really weren't so frequent as to warrant a vigil.

After some time, Kurt asks, "Do you receive news from Vienna?"

"There is hardly anyone there anymore."

"Yes."

Oskar shrugs his shoulders to his wife as she risks returning to the room. He listens to the quiet phone line, "Kurt?"

"Good-bye, Oskar."

"Good-bye."

The urge to phone Oskar again rises as soon as Kurt returns the receiver but he resists for a few minutes. For a while he organizes all the laundry receipts, flyers, old letters, vouchers, and other random detritus he saves. The slips of paper annoy him. He feels buried, hampered by obligation but unable to ignore even the smallest detail, unable to advance in even the most trivial of tasks except through the most exhaustive series of logical steps. He has to attend to every stage in every process at the expense of his work and of his good humor. When the papers are logically ordered, he phones Oskar. "Do you remember Olga Hahn-Neurath?"

As Adele leaves the house, she shouts, "I'll be happy to drive without having a genius in the car," but knows she isn't loud enough for him to hear. She likes to say this, for instance, when she drives the Morgensterns home after a visit. "I'm so happy to drive without having a genius in the car, you can't know," she'd say in German to Oskar's irritated image in the rearview mirror while his wife Dorothy would turn with raised eyebrows to glare out the passenger seat window.

But today, for whatever reason, she returns the keys to her pocket as she passes the car in the drive and walks the few blocks to the local grocer. She tries to avoid any unnecessary chatting with the cashier, since her own poor English still makes her feel quite ashamed. Without a word, she pays for the single piece of fruit she has carefully selected. Every previous selection on every previous day for several months has been rejected. She chooses, or so it seems to her she chooses, an apple that is small so as not to intimidate him, that is pale red so as not to seem unnatural or tainted, and that retains a stump from the stem for no reason at all. She clomps home from the store, the apple in hand, her thighs heavier than they used to be. They feel big and round as they push the street away, kicking the cement and earth behind her. The waistband of her pantyhose has become a punishing wire with no natural resting place. And there is absolutely no accommodating the white cotton diamond crotch, which usually aligns with one thigh like a poorly applied giant gauze. Her stockings bunch over the front of her thigh and down the back with each stride like a kind of knitting stitch. Her flesh rolls around until the nylon twists and cuts, piano-wire sharp. She catches her hefty reflection in a sparkling shop window. "Pff," she whistles, a tune of simultaneous self-pity and acceptance. She thinks: *My thighs are plump like an engorged Florida orange. Peeled. Like a plump, peeled, engorged Florida orange.* Produce is on her mind.

Through the window Kurt watches Adele return from the corner store and squat over a hedge decorated by a plastic pink flamingo she has installed in their front lawn. She was impressed with the nativity scenes that appeared in the neighborhood last December and wanted an ornament of her own. *It is awfully charming,* Gödel agreed. She gives up on the garden and waddles through the door. She is tired. Her hair has come loose from the blindly placed clips and her glasses have lost their grip. She pries off her pantyhose and leaves them dangling over the back of a green vinyl kitchen chair. As she has taken up smoking, she stops in the kitchen to light an immaculately machine-rolled cigarette she finds in the tobacco-collecting pocket of her dark jacket that she has not yet removed. She extends her lower lip in a pucker to blow the smoke straight up to her eyes, a vague blue-gray complement to her definite blue gray-eyes. She smokes the cigarette down to the burning foam and stubs out the filter. In the study, just as she left him, she finds Kurt, the child she never had, and brings him his apple.

He inspects the thick hide of the little red fruit. The skin is puckered and marked and browning around the dimple where it was torn from the vine. He looks for proof of distress, punctures, evidence that the storekeeper is colluding with the doctors to poison him. That mark there, too deep, too clean to be natural. He throws it away. He will ask her for another apple tomorrow and the day after and the day after as he did the day before and the day before that. Each day he will throw the poisoned fruit away.

"Why, Kurtele?" She shouts at the discarded fruit, both arms extended plaintively, fingers spread, bag strap weighing one arm lower than the other in the dark coat she still hasn't removed.

He ignores her question. "The radiator unit you bought from Sears is emanating poison gases. The smell is trapped in my nose and clinging to the hairs. I have called Sears to have it removed."

"Removed? We will freeze all winter. Again! You want us to freeze all winter?"

"Adele, it is bad for my heart."

"There is nothing wrong with your heart, Kurtele. The doctors swear to it. They have checked a hundred times. Your heart is fine, just fine," she gestures in front of him as if to dust away the very idea. "And nobody is going to poison you."

"*You* nearly poisoned me in Vienna with coal. Now with the radiator?"

"That was an accident, Kurtele," she says with the exasperation of one who has repeated the same defense so many times that the phrase has become its own word, an independent concept emerging larger than the sum of its parts. "That was an accident, Kurtele!"

"I will taste it for you," she says fishing the blemished fruit from the garbage and breaking the skin with her front teeth. Adele eats the rest of the apple. As she licks her fingers clean, she throws the core back into the pail.

As the afternoon wears on Adele peels stringy meat from a carcass and with it some veins and ligaments tear free leaving a smooth clean arc of cartilage. The purple flesh stinks of liquefied fat and the grease shines on Adele's calloused fingers as she pushes the strips of chicken into the steaming stew. Kurt has been in his study all day. He can't bear the smell or sight of cooking animal flesh. The texture of meat sliding along his tongue repulses him. She will have to puree the stew and cajole him to eat. First he will watch her taste the hot soup to demonstrate that the food is not poisoned. Then he will watch her eat an entire bowl and wait at least one hour just to be certain there are no slow-acting agents in the brew. If she is lucky he will allow her to feed him spoonful by spoonful like a baby. That would be a successful dinner.

She is sweating from leaning over the stove. Or maybe she has contracted that strain of influenza that wafts through New

Jersey each year. It is only July but it's possible. She must not let on to Kurt that she isn't well. If he sees her perspire near the kitchen he will not eat for days. Before she calls him to witness her tasting of the food, she scrubs her hands with wobbling vigor, then tucks the well-defined curls under and around her head and ears. She mops her face dry and stands at the small oval mirror in the hall to reapply eyebrow pencil in a straight line that moves up as it moves out. It makes her look slightly angry but it also gives her eyes a bit of a lift. Standing in a three-quarters pose so the port-wine-stain birthmark is almost hidden she thinks, *Even fat, I can still look good.* She whistles, "Pff," and then booms, "Kurtele. Soup."

It is not destined to be a successful dinner. As Kurt fights his dark mood and watches Adele demonstrate the restorative powers of the untainted soup, her face oils with perspiration. She tries to talk through the intensifying nausea and pain so as not to alarm her husband but collapses midway through a running commentary on Oskar's wife and her putative obsession with ginger ale.

The ensuing hour is a disaster. Kurt yells to her. He is afraid to touch her or the soup that has spilled across her arm and onto the linoleum. He feels old. He feels wretched. For a few minutes he cannot bear the idea of anyone seeing them like this so he does nothing. Finally he panics. There are several confused calls to Oskar and eventually Dorothy grabs the receiver from her husband, hangs up on Kurt, and calls for an ambulance.

Adele is rushed to the hospital where an emergency colostomy is performed in which a section of bowel tissue near the end of her small intestine is passed through the abdominal wall to join an incision in the skin of her belly. The sides of her intestine are sewn to the abdominal wall and an artificial bag is taped to the opening to collect the stool, which is looser and softer than she had imagined. She has grown accustomed to checking Kurt's stool at his insistence although she never had more than a passing interest in her own. She protects Kurt from the sight of her colostomy bag but the idea alone infests him so that he is relieved that no such foul semisolids have passed through him for several days. Kurt spends as many hours by her side as the nurses allow, doting as best he can on his pretty, sweet Adele. He would sleep by her side if the staff allowed it. And so five months of her convalescence pass.

No one is sure how Kurt survives these five months. Adele's collapse makes eating of any kind unthinkable for many days. Adele tries her best to convince him the soup was not poisoned but Kurt insists an acrid breath came off the broth. Oskar tries too. He explains in medical terms, "It was a simple obstruction of the bowel, not uncommon in high-fat diets." Adele tries half-heartedly to force him to eat her hospital food, which is so poor that even she has trouble getting it down—although she has developed a hankering for Tuesday's mashed potatoes and peas. In time he begins to eat extremely modestly—not enough to keep him alive, but just enough to delay his death. And so Kurt starves. A very slow and very painful starvation.

Adele's colostomy episode has destroyed Kurt's regulation of food versus laxative. His diary of bowel movements, body temperature, and medicinal intake becomes erratic and unchartable without Adele there to wake him, bathe him, send him off to sleep. Her side of the bed is empty and still. He can see the phantom shadow that was once Adele rolling in the rough sheets. He can still inhale the remnant of her last musky sleep in their bed and he strains to hear her daybreak sighs. But her side of the bed is empty.

"Bring me cyanide!" Kurt begs Oskar over the phone. "They come into my room every night and inject me with a yellow serum. What are they doing to me? Oskar, you must help me kill myself. Please Oskar, I beg you to help me. Adele's doctors will commit me to an asylum. They poisoned the chicken. Oskar—bring me cyanide!"

"Who comes into your room? Who?" Oskar bellows into the phone only to realize the line has gone dead. "He's from another world," he tells his wife by way of explanation. "Cyanide, he asks me for cyanide. What, to poison his own food? Do you know where he gets that from? Snow White's poisoned apple. It's his favorite movie." The abrupt blaring of the dial tone has further battered Oskar's spirits. "Dorothy, you know he can be splendidly charming at times. Animated and quite funny. He has been good, sharp company for me all these years, and you remember how Einstein valued his friendship.

You have no idea what such a conversation means for me: here is one of the most brilliant men of our century, greatly attached to me. He is clearly suffering from some kind of paranoia, expecting help from me, and I am unable to extend it to him. By clinging to me—and he has nobody else, that is quite clear—he adds to the burden I am carrying."

When Kurt arrives at his door an hour after the third phone call that day, Oskar is unable to camouflage his dismay at Kurt's cadaverous appearance, obvious despite the padding of several layers of clothes. His skin is green where it's thickest and pulled tautest against his cheekbones, paling to a tough yellow hide around the holes in the skull where a space is left for his eyes. His temples are flaccid and broad as saucers. "The funny thing," Oskar once told his wife, "is that Adele is a good cook if what you crave is traditional German fare."

Kurt's hosts place a sizzling ginger ale over ice on the table in front of him. The glass is half full of ginger root syrup and sparkly water with lots of yellow pulp from the previous occupant of the glass—an orange juice spritzer. The top half of the glass is loaded with sun, hot heavy sun coming in from the window, as though the star drooled a liquid along its rays into the cup. The heat is causing the ginger root and sparkling water to froth. The last time they visited the Morgensterns as a couple, Adele drank three of their homemade ginger ales. Her face muffled in the glass, she sucked the sizzling juice down to the heavy glass base. The beverage became a thirst-enhancing syrup that lined her teeth and tongue and all the tubing down to her longing-for-some-water stomach. When she expressed her thirst, Mrs. Morgenstern misunderstood and brought her another homemade ginger ale over ice. And then another. Her gluttony made a bad impression on the Morgensterns, and her hosts' inability to supply a little fresh water made no great impression on Adele either. The two women sat across from each other and began an exhausting volley of feminine poses, each intending to outdo the other. Adele stretched the hem of her skirt as she wriggled to the edge of the sofa in what she imagined to be a more feline perch. To which Dorothy responded with a quaint crossing of the ankles. To which Adele rested her big hands on her knees and tucked in her chin, trying to suck all of her corpulence into a more elongated shape, even pushing her hand hopefully on her middle. To which Dorothy angled her wrists delicately to the side of her knees. And so the evening went on, each matching the other's posture and then raising the stakes one ridiculous step at a time.

Adele managed to eke conversational material out of the ginger-ale episode for months. The sight of the very same beverage in Adele's absence only magnifies Kurt's loneliness. Thus the visit does not begin well. Oskar and his wife suggest that, what with the seventy-degree weather, Kurt should remove his sweater, not suspecting the presence of another sweater under that. But Kurt can't shake the chill and accepts instead another knit from Oskar's wife. And then a coat. And then another coat. And a warm wrap. And then, with difficulty, Oskar lights a fire despite his own discomfort. The process of draping fabrics over the visiting cadaver consumes the better part of their meeting.

Kurt is incredibly transparent. "You're worried. You have worried eyes," Oskar says and scoops his forefinger and thumb around his own to illustrate the locus of worried eyes. "Yes. And I am tired." Desperation blows across his face. Oskar frowns, as he sees the storm forming, his own face nearly as transparent as Kurt's.

Kurt steels himself for a painful moment of self-awareness. He is a skeletal puppet in abundant costume, theatrically lit by a fire that manages to overpower the yellow sunlight. "Oskar," he says to get his attention, as if it is Oskar who is lost in a dangerous maze of his own thoughts. "Oskar, I never lived up to my potential. Not after I came to America."

Oskar strokes his forehead and searches for some consoling words. He finds none.

"If I had not discovered the incompleteness theorems, someone else would have."

"I doubt that." Oskar holds his breath as he readjusts his legs.

"Yes, someone would have because mathematics exists independently of any of us."

"I know many clever people, Kurt, brilliant people. I do not know anyone who could have done what you did. I'm sure we still haven't fully understood the implications, I'm sure we haven't. But we all know you discovered the ultimate limit. Einstein showed that nothing can travel faster than light, Heisenberg realized that we can never transcend quantum uncertainty, and you taught us that numbers, *numbers even,* are forever beyond human reason."

"I am not so famous."

"Does that matter so much?"

"It matters if the ideas are not well known."

"But your ideas are known. You have changed everything. And now there are machines and maybe one day intelligence, artificial intelligence." If it sounds trite to add, "What an impact to have on our future," Oskar does so only because he means it and he says it almost to himself.

"Wittgenstein said my theorems were no better than tricks. Trickery. *Kunststücke!*"

"Wittgenstein," Oskar laughs. His name still stirs memories of Vienna. Although they have petered off as of late, Oskar has tolerated many a tirade about Wittgenstein—about his possession of Moritz, his ideas, and worst of all his disregard of Kurt's achievements. "You well know," here he pounds on his chair to instill a point he has made countless times; "you well know," he repeats, "that there are many who consider your proof to be the most important result in the history of mathematics."

They are quiet just long enough for the sun to perceptibly change angles before Kurt says, "I am still capable of some feats. I still have that ability."

"I have no doubt."

"I am making real choices, incredible choices."

"It's these choices you make that scare me."

"These actions of mine are a show of strength, you know, a demonstration of freedom. A proof of free will."

"Which choices exactly?"

"I haven't eaten in over a week."

"Jesus, Kurt."

"Every force in the universe drives us into these seemingly inescapable cycles. Every force accounted for. I am doing the impossible. I am choosing to disobey these forces, to react differently than they instruct."

"Jesus, Kurt," Oskar repeats.

That was their last real exchange before Kurt was lost among hallucinations. Oskar tries to find a path through Kurt's mind that will lead him to where his brilliant friend is hiding. He would take him by the hand and bring him forward out the portals of his eyes, through the binocular lenses in the round black frames, to this simple reality. The conversation is torture. (There will be many other terrible conversations with repeating themes. Kurt will phone relentlessly for two more weeks until the day a heartbroken Dorothy answers—the day Oskar dies. Gödel will hang up on her without a word. He will speak of it to no one. Who knows what's real?) Unable to get up on his useless legs, Oskar remains seated as he hears the door close after Kurt, who departs into the humid day with the Morgensterns' two coats and one sweater, leaving the wrap where it falls on the floor. From his wheelchair, Oskar reaches for a flat iron poker and snuffs out the fire.

Adele returns home near Christmas, enfeebled and confined to bed. She cannot nurse Kurt's atrophied body and overzealous mind, so that one swells at the cost of the other. The meat burns off his bones and the marrow dries inside until all that is left is the fragile skeletal shell. She wails in hysterics until Kurt finally concedes to admit himself to the hospital as an emergency case.

He spends his last days sitting upright in a hospital chair, mortified by the agony. He misdiagnoses every joint-crunching ache, every contraction in his chest, every cramp in his side. He suspects a heart damaged by childhood fever, an ulcer aggravated by tea, organ damage from poisoned food. But really it is just the frantic pleas from all of the elements of his body—appeals for mercy from their murderer.

For three days he sits in that hospital chair at sixty-five pounds, recalcitrant and taciturn, until death comes from prolonged self-starvation. He believes this suicide to be a triumph of his free will, an impossible choice imposed against all rightful forces. But from the outside, his suicide could seem to be the only possible outcome of two drives finding equal strength: the ultimate impasse between the determination to live and the determination to die. Could it be that his choice is not a choice, only an illusion?

For these three days he fights off doubts and fears that there is no soul, no hereafter, and the mind is no more than a biological mechanism that dies when it dies and that is that. He spends these three days turned inward, focused with the full effort of his ailing mind.

WILMSLOW, 1954

The reasons behind people's actions interest Alan very little. We are rarely interested in things we are no good at and Alan is no good at deciphering people, not even himself. When he boards an early train from Manchester to London this morning with the intention of alighting in Buckinghamshire, he never stops to consider his motives and so he never stops to worry over the implications. Two years ago he distinctly remembers deciding it was time to go back to the woods and find his wartime investment. He even went so far as to acquire proper tools for locating the lost bounty but they languished in his shed along with his war medal. When sleep deserted him last night and he found his electroplating experiment too boring to alleviate his mood, the idea of the trip to the woods came to him all at once. Who knows why? Maybe he was the littlest bit sentimental for that time when he was the littlest bit happy.

The early morning trip is easy, his fatigue almost pleasant, as he rocks past rows of attached brick houses. Alan makes his way to the woods and sets his expedition for the silver bars under way. By noon, he is digging in the mud. He is relaxed, if depressed. His body disgusts him. He is obese and impotent. Most horrid of all, he has developed breasts from the hormones. These have been changes that he finally admits are both permanent and impossible. They have poisoned him. They've as good as killed him. If they don't finish the job, he'll do it himself.

After all of these years the pram is still in the woods. It has collected seasons of rain and detritus, rarely having a chance to dry out. It created its own microclimate and grows a rich culture of mold and vegetation. Joan would know what these species are called. The navy blue canvas is now black and green with speckles of powdery blue in places. The metal spokes of the big wheels stick out from mossy centers like perfect, shiny, metal twigs. Much of its artificial character has been worn down so that it looks like something grown naturally. The pram is a peculiar landmark, a gravestone of sorts.

This is his third and final expedition to recover the bars. The first time he managed to locate 200 pounds in prewar notes that he buried alongside the silver. The notes were soiled but usable. The second time he came with a metal detector of his own design and manufacture. It worked well enough to call up several metal bits and bobs just under the soil but not well enough to see even as deep as the shallow grave in the floor of the woods where he buried the first bar. The second bar he was fairly sure he had located under the bed of the stream. There it remained when digging was discouraged by the depth of the icy cold water.

This time he comes back with an industrial metal detector that turns up yet more conducting debris (Where does it all come from? The sky?), but still fails to isolate the first silver bar. The second bar is truly lost. The original bridge has been torn down, replaced with a new structure, and concrete now lines the streambed. The Benzedrine inhaler with the enciphered instructions fell along with the original bridge. While one of the builders spotted it with amazement he discarded the mystery in the rubble, along with his curiosity. The second bar was never found and must still lie there, neither rotting nor fertilizing. An unnaturally shiny bone.

Alan isn't too disappointed. When he abandons the search, he commits to getting really filthy. He climbs and digs and skips and romps like a child. He searches for worms and fractal roots until the day is gone.

He travels the long way back to Manchester, facing backward as the train rocks and sways while it tears past the countryside. The trees and hills stream away like rain sloughing off an umbrella. The scenery smearing on the other side of the bubble of glass. In its reflection he sees his own blue-eyed windowpanes and he feels himself on the outside of the impenetrable indigo marbles that separate him from the world. He looks out from behind these eyes, permanently locked in, to stare with futility into those eyes, permanently locked out.

For the first time in the two years since the trial he recognizes himself in those eyes, unchanged as they are by hormones, fat, and breasts. The trial, incidentally, was quick and decisive. Alan and his accomplice both pleaded guilty to the twelve charges of Gross Indecency. (Yes, Alan confessed, he did it. No, he did not believe it was wrong.) The several weeks between his arrest and trial were a torment of nervous agitation although in Alan this surfaced as only a mild deepening of his already unusual manner. He worked at home as best he could, occasionally appearing at the university or in London for a conference. Ostracism and embarrassment being familiar states for him, he seemed to go on with life and even laugh—almost boast—of his crimes. But privately panic had seized him—a panic that would spread steadily throughout his system.

His lawyer explained that the sentence imposed for Gross Indecency contrary to Section 11 of the Criminal Law Amendment Act 1885 was either castration or prison. Alan was still resentful over his circumcision. The prospect of losing the ballasts, the primary culprits as it were, was entirely impossible. He would definitely opt for prison. Prison he could handle—cruelty, bullying, abusive hierarchies—he had been trained for this at Sherborne School for boys in Dorset. He wouldn't handle it *well.* He'd be a disaster—but he'd survive and with his manhood attached.

At first, when he heard his lawyer use the word, it was as though the incision had been made. He was felled before the sentence's end. As his knees gave way, the blood raced to his groin in hysterical support, his lips and pores not benefiting from the blood loss. "Can they do that?" he managed. Through a metallic orchestra of cardiovascular mania he could almost make out the matter-of-factly recited catalog of cases resolved by castration, the technique applied liberally in America not to mention the recent article in the *Times* advocating the broad implementation of the practice to rectify perverts and deviants. He could barely hear over the roar in his ears. The precise phrasing didn't matter. It wasn't poetry. He understood that once again he hadn't understood. And this time they weren't just going to shove him below the floorboards.

"They might as well kill me." He watched himself in the window over the lawyer's shoulder. The reflection of the lights tinted his jaw and reminded him of the drool of blood, the sight of which had knocked him unconscious all those years ago during the war, and he actually cackled—high, piercing, and ridiculous. "You know I faint at the sight of blood," he blurted. The laugh continued, pinched through his sealed mouth as he tried to repress his nervousness, about as successfully as he repressed his sexuality.

In the end he was not surgically castrated but chemically castrated with massive doses of estrogen that left him impotent and with notably developed breasts. His sentence required he submit to treatments at regular intervals, receiving his pills at the Manchester Royal Infirmary with a final hormone implant that was reputed to last for three months. Not taking any chances, Alan had the implant surgically removed at the end of his sentence and with that he was finally, at least in the eyes of the law, free. Although he wasn't often given to self-pity or cynicism, he rather suspected that this was not exactly true.

Two years after the trial and one year after the removal of his hormone implant, the effects feel irreversible. His libido was never entirely obliterated and there was the occasional affair he managed abroad, in Paris or Norway, with the usual gratifying combination of disaster and comedy. But in truth, the organotherapy has corroded him. His flesh is jelly and his desires have softened to a jelly too.

He doesn't know how to voice his humiliation or even how to experience it. It rattles around in him like a broken part, dislodged and loose in his metal frame. The humiliation won't settle on one place, sink in where it would no doubt fester but at least could be quarantined and possibly even treated. If not steadily eroded by the imperceptible buffing waves of time, then maybe more aggressively targeted, excised by his Jungian analyst. But the shame just won't burrow and bind.

The train returns him to Manchester from his final, failed attempt to recover his silver bars. In the isolation of his Wilmslow home, he discards his muddy clothes in a laundry hamper and twists the taps to the bath, which squeak and complain before dribbling tepid water into the shallow tub. He immerses as much of himself as he can. His knees, still high in the cool air, are covered with goose pimples. As he looks over his limp flesh, the yellow folds at the edges of his unfamiliar body, the undulation of the excess skin trapping an unnatural accumulation of oily lard, it finally happens. His humiliation takes root, furrows deep into the fat of his engorged breasts, and from that stronghold emits a pulse of red raw shame. It takes one full day for the tender pink to fade and even then it disperses only reluctantly when his body goes cold and dead.

He steps out of the water, half dries himself, and silently begins the design of his suicide as he hums his favorite fairy tale, *Dip the apple in the brew, let the sleeping death seep through.*

It doesn't occur to him to write a note. He doesn't clean up or place any ominous phone calls. Remorse for his mother hinders him for a bit and he allows himself to wonder about this on into the darkness. Late that night he manages a solution to the problem of his mother and within minutes he is supple as butter and deliciously succumbs to woozy sleep. He wakes early with anticipation over the chemistry experiment he needs to prepare. He wakes early, but from his slumber to the end of his life he is fluid and at ease.

It is potassium cyanide that he has on hand. It is an element in his electroplating experiment. Ingested, cyanide induces cellular asphyxiation. Each cell will suffocate and as he is just a collection of cells, he will suffocate with them. A bag of minerals seeped in history's soil. No hereafter. No soul. No God.

When he was a student at Sherborne, he tried a similar electroplating experiment. Even back then, the materials inspired a morbid plan to kill himself, using cyanide, an apple, and an electric current. It would have been fun in a way, at least the execution of the experiment, if not the actual dying part. He wonders what would have happened if he had chosen suicide as a schoolboy in Sherborne. How all the events in the universe, big and small, collude to make the world exactly as it is. How all of his ideas and actions, big and small, are necessary steps in an even bigger mechanism. But then he couldn't have made any choices different from the ones he made, because there is no such thing as free will. The world is exactly as it is.

And still it astounds him how much he feels that he is making choices.

He almost did succeed in killing himself at Sherborne quite by accident several weeks after the worst gloom ebbed and he felt almost stable. The day after his release from beneath the floorboards, he took the seat next to Chris in chemistry instruction and began to tell him how he had reproduced the iodine experiment even though the color never seemed quite right and the beaker smashed on the floor. (Chris could not help but remark on the coincidence of Alan's appearance on the seat next to him in each and every lecture. Alan had no defense and feared some reproach. But after class, when he trailed behind Chris on their way to religious instruction, he felt better, since Chris beckoned him to follow—he did so with his eyes.) When he then took the seat next to Chris in religious instruction, Alan invited him to see his more elaborate cyanide experiment for electroplating metal. It wasn't strictly allowed to fraternize with boys of another house in one's room, but then it wasn't strictly forbidden either. By midnight he admitted that Chris was not going to call around after supper as he had been invited to do. In the comfort of the soft fold of his arm, his face sizzled under fruit-sized tears that boiled off and dried to mineral salt on his stinging jaw. Alan was drenched in loneliness so viscous he couldn't believe it wasn't an actual substance.

Every night at school he ate an apple, except that night and the subsequent eleven nights. Instead, he dismantled his experiment and reassembled the pieces, including his habitual late-night fruit, into a suicide machine—an electrified poison apple. Several times over the coming weeks he dismantled and reassembled the morbid contraption. Every few days he would rub the rippled skin of the souring fruit. Blank hours moved past the room until morning when he threw the toxic apple in the rubbish, recovering a fresh piece at breakfast with which to rebuild the apparatus.

After eleven days, Chris came to Turing's room with a new article on mathematics that he had to share with old Turing. Alan quickly dismantled his inventive death appliance, tossing the apple aside. That night he thought about Chris and proof and truth and meaning and faith and he didn't feel quite so hollow. Which is why he found it particularly hilarious that, when he found an apple in his pile of bedding, he absentmindedly lifted it to his lips to take a bite. *Wash your hands,* his mother used to scold. *Don't put them in your mouth,* she'd warn. *One day you'll poison yourself.*

Anytime he feels like this—blank, empty, numb, dumb—he thinks of that hour under the floor and of Chris. It is his brain's involuntary response, like an unwelcome bittersweet memory that invades his thoughts in reaction to a sentimental odor—the smell of his childhood. And every time, it almost makes him laugh.

He stares into the clear beaker of poison until the memory of Chris has come and gone. He dips the apple in the brew and returns it to its place on the table. It will take only a few minutes. He doesn't know if he should lie or fall. He rather wants to lie down first and arranges himself on the bed. He lies there a while. It does feel good. The new heaviness in his belly and arms doesn't bother him when he's sunk in the bed like this, the extra flesh pushing him deeper into the springs. He lies there a long while.

When the time comes, as it seems to, flowing by until he is carried on its relentless current, he sits on the edge of the metal-framed bed, reaches for the apple, and breaks the pretty red skin with his teeth. It is mealy. He bites again with a mouth still full of masticated fruit. He tries to stand. He lurches and swallows as he falls.

His cells don't die in unison. Each cell perishes separately like a bug squashed between two calloused fingers. Some systems shut down immediately while others kick and jolt. He can feel his back connected to the floor until the skin is so cold he thinks it must be gone. He can feel a vicious itch on his left thigh and his right foot jerks.

He imagined he'd have one last thought and wondered what it would be. It starts with Bold Blue, Chris, An Ache of Love, Crushed Glass. Then his mind folds up like a de-tuning orchestra and while he remains aware and aware of himself, his thoughts begin to disintegrate into component parts until language is gone and there is just abstraction. His last thought isn't a word or an image; it is a bolt in his mind as his brain releases and every dominion of his gray matter throws out a last note that rings as long as the chemicals can sustain it like the resonance of an opera long after the orchestra stops playing.

A froth gathers around his lips and bubbles delicately in the breeze of his last exhalation.

NEW YORK CITY

Here I am, in New York City. It is the twenty-first century. This place is as good a place, this time as good a time, as any.

I am stepping off a curb. The subway entrance is just across the street. Big green orbs signify that the downtown entrance is open. Artificial light competing against the sun. There are children in the park; a woman with silver hair and a long, old coat; a couple on a bench. A yellow plague of taxis infests the streets. I walk behind some and in front of others. We all move along fixed trajectories, following our prescribed arcs. The plague disappears behind the stone wall as the old steps take me down into the subway.

I am under the city. In this stink of an underground, miscellaneous liquids pour from the streets off the grating and onto the tracks. A train comes. The car is empty. I can see my eye in the window of the C train. A big black eye. I'm inside looking out and outside looking in. I stare into the opaque disk at a biological machine.

There is no ending. I've tried to invent one but it was a lie and I don't want to be a liar. This story will end where it began, in the middle. A triangle or a circle. A closed loop with three points. A wayfaring chronicle searching for a treasure buried in the woods, on the streets, in books, on empty trains. Craving an amulet, a jewel, a reason, a purpose, a truth. I can almost see it on the periphery, just where they said it would be, glistening at me from the far edges of every angle I search.

NOTES

It is natural when reading an account of historical figures to wonder which, if any, central facts have been changed. The scenes that structure the present work were drawn from the technical writings of Kurt Gödel and Alan Turing, their archived papers, and their biographies. For biographical information, I am indebted to three books in particular, *Alan Turing: The Enigma,* by Andrew Hodges; *Logical Dilemmas: The Life and Work of Kurt Gödel,* by John Dawson; and *Ludwig Wittgenstein: The Duty of a Genius,* by Ray Monk.

The number of facts that were intentionally altered in this narrative is small. The most liberty was taken with secondary characters. For instance, Otto Neurath and Olga Hahn-Neurath were indeed part of the Vienna Circle. Otto had red hair and a red beard and a warm, burly personality. Olga was blind and smoked cigars. But I am not privy to the details of their friendship with Gödel, and the story of their friendship as told here is largely invented. It was not Oskar who waved good-bye as Gödel traveled on the *Champlain* back to Europe but another colleague—although Oskar was to become Gödel's last living friend and the other details of that friendship recounted in this story have historical support. Turing first went to see *Snow White* with a Cambridge friend, not Joan, and the timing of the trips to recover the silver in the woods, as well as his visit to the Gypsy Queen, were altered for cohesion. Another point worth mentioning: Turing's remarkable 1936 paper, "On Computable Numbers, with an Application to the Entscheidungsproblem," is often discussed in the context of the Halting Problem. However, Turing did not use this language—the expression was coined in the 1950s—and so that language is not used explicitly in this book. The depth and magnitude of both Turing's and Gödel's ideas are only barely touched upon here. I can only defer to the numerous excellent volumes devoted to their work. Last, there are many omissions, fascinating particulars of Gödel's and Turing's lives that are beyond the scope of this book. A list of such particulars includes Gödel's friendship with Einstein as well as Turing's work in the United States during the war and his postwar development of the Manchester computer.

As for the included details and this story as a whole, they are a response to documented historical events. Turing had been trapped beneath the floorboards at Sherborne School at least once. He cracked the Enigma code, buried silver bullion in the woods during the war, was engaged to Joan Clarke, had that ill-fated affair with Arnold Murray, endured the subsequent hormone therapy, visited the Gypsy Queen, and committed suicide with a bite from a cyanide-laden apple. Gödel did marry Adele and she did spoon-feed him homemade German fare. He did believe in the transmigration of the soul, spent time in various sanatoria, suffered from paranoia and delusions, saved scraps of paper and volumes of notebooks covered front and back, and ultimately starved himself to death.

There are several places in the present work where direct quotations appear, although the context may have been changed. These notes identify and restore any full quotes and place them into their original context with references. In most cases a primary reference is cited as well as a secondary reference in which the quote can be found. This is in no way a complete list of sources consulted.

16 "Undeniably he is not a 'normal' boy." Comments on Turing's school reports from Geoffrey O'Hanlon, the housemaster of Westcott house at Sherborne School. Andrew Hodges, *Alan Turing: The Enigma* (New York: Simon & Schuster, 1983).
27 "I cannot forgive the stupidity of his attitude towards sane discussion on the New Testament." Comments of Alan Turing's formmaster, A. H. Trelawny Ross. Hodges, *Alan Turing.*
71 "Half the lies they tell about me are true." Raymond Smullyan lists several self-annihilating sentences first compiled by Dr. Saul Gorn in his "Compendium of Rarely Used Clichés." Raymond Smullyan, *5000 B.C. and Other Philosophical Fantasies* (New York: St Martin's Press, 1983).
99 "My dear Mrs. Morcom, I was so pleased to be at the Clockhouse for Easter. I always like to think of it specially in connection with Chris. It reminds us that Chris is in some way alive *now.* One is perhaps too inclined to think only of him alive at some future time when we shall meet him again; but it is really so much more helpful to think of him as just separated from us for the present." Alan Turing to Mrs. Morcom. Hodges, *Alan Turing.*
101 "It used to be supposed in Science that if everything was known about the Universe at any particular moment then we can predict what it will be through all the future. This idea was really due to the great success of astronomical prediction. More modern science however has come to the conclusion that when we are dealing with atoms and electrons we are quite unable to know the exact state of them; our instruments being made of atoms and electrons them-

selves. The conception then of being able to know the exact state of the universe then really must break down on the small scale. This means then that the theory which held that as eclipses etc. are predestined so were all our actions breaks down too. We have a will which is able to determine the action of the atoms probably in a small portion of the brain, or possibly all over it. . . . When the body is asleep I cannot guess what happens but when the body dies the 'mechanism' of the body, holding the spirit, is gone and the spirit finds a new body sooner or later perhaps immediately." Alan Turing to Mrs. Morcom. Hodges, *Alan Turing.*

112 "The coffee is wretched." Gödel's comment to Oskar in response to Oskar's query about Vienna. Diaries of Oskar Morgenstern, Perkins Memorial Library of Duke University. John W. Dawson, *Logical Dilemmas: The Life and Work of Kurt Gödel* (Wellesley, Mass.: A. K. Peters, 1997).

112 "What brings you to America, Herr Bergmann?" Kurt Gödel to Gustav Bergmann as relayed by Bergmann to John Dawson. Dawson, *Logical Dilemmas.*

118 "You remind me of someone who is looking through a closed window and cannot explain to himself the strange movements of a passer-by. He doesn't know what kind of storm is raging outside and that this person is perhaps only with great effort keeping himself on his feet." Ludwig Wittgenstein to his sister Hermine Wittgenstein. Hermine Wittgenstein, "My Brother Ludwig," in *Ludwig Wittgenstein: Personal Recollections,* ed. Rush Rhees (Oxford: Basil Blackwell, 1981).

123 "Superstition brings bad luck." Raymond Smullyan lists several self-annihilating sentences first compiled by Dr. Saul Gorn. This expression is number 13 on that list. Smullyan, *5000 B.C. and Other Philosophical Fantasies.*

134–35 Conversation between Wittgenstein and Turing in Wittgenstein's 1939 course Foundations of Mathematics, as recorded in students' notes during lecture XXI:

WITTGENSTEIN: "Think of the case of the Liar. It is very queer in a way that this should have puzzled anyone—much more extraordinary than you might think: that this should be the thing to worry human beings. Because the thing works like this: if a man says 'I am lying' we say that it follows that he is not lying, from which it follows that he is lying and so on. Well, so what? You can go on like that until you are black in the face. Why not? It doesn't matter. . . . Now suppose a man says 'I am lying' and I say 'Therefore you are not, therefore you are, therefore you are not . . . '—What is wrong? Nothing. Except that it is of no use; it is just a useless language-game, and why should anyone be excited?"

TURING: "What puzzles one is that one usually uses a contradiction as a criterion for having done something wrong. But in this case one cannot find anything done wrong."

WITTGENSTEIN: "Yes—and more: nothing has been done wrong. Where will the harm come?"

And then later in the lecture:

TURING: "The real harm will not come in unless there is an application, in which case a bridge may fall down or something of that sort."

WITTGENSTEIN: "Ah, now this idea of a bridge falling down if there is a contradiction is of immense importance. But I am too stupid to begin it now; so I will go into it next time."

And then during lecture XXII:

WITTGENSTEIN: "The question is: Why are people afraid of contradictions? It is easy to understand why they should

> be afraid of contradictions in orders, descriptions, etc., outside of mathematics. The question is: Why should they be afraid of contradictions inside mathematics? Turing says, 'Because something may go wrong with the application.' But nothing need go wrong. And if something does go wrong—if the bridge breaks down—then your mistake was of the kind of using a wrong natural law."

Ludwig Wittgenstein, *Wittgenstein's Lectures on the Foundations of Mathematics, Cambridge 1939, From the Notes of R. G. Bosanquet, Norman Malcolm, Rush Rhees, and Yorick Smythies,* ed. Cora Diamond (New York: Cornell University Press, 1976).

166 "Church is here of course, but Gödel, Kleene, Rosser and Bernays who were here last year have left. I don't think I mind very much missing any of these except Gödel." Turing in a letter home from Princeton. Hodges, *Alan Turing.*

166 "I would say that fair play must be given to the machine. Instead of it sometimes giving no answer we could arrange that it gives occasional wrong answers. But the human mathematician would likewise make blunders when trying out new techniques. It is easy for us to regard these blunders as not counting and give him another chance, but the machine would probably be allowed no mercy. In other words then, if a machine is expected to be infallible, it cannot also be intelligent. There are several theorems which say almost exactly that. But these theorems say nothing about how much intelligence may be displayed if a machine makes no pretence at infallibility. . . . The machine must be allowed to have contact with human beings in order that it may adapt itself to their standards. The game of chess may perhaps be rather suitable for this purpose, as the moves of the opponent will automatically provide this contact." Turing in a talk to the London Mathematical Society. Hodges, *Alan Turing.*

173–74 "He's about twenty-five years of age, five foot ten inches, with black hair."

"We have reason to believe your description is false. Why are you lying?"

"Would you care to tell us what kind of an affair you have had with him?"

"a lovely statement . . . a flowing style, almost like prose."

"beyond them in some of its phraseology."

Pieces of the exchange between Alan Turing and the detectives Mr. Wills and Mr. Rimmer as recorded in documents of Chester Record Office. Hodges, *Alan Turing.*

175 "I suppose you know I'm a homosexual." Alan Turing in a letter to his brother John. Hodges, *Alan Turing.*

175 "When you come to Liverpool perhaps you will stop off to see me in jail." Alan Turing in a letter to Fred Clayton, a Cambridge friend. Hodges, *Alan Turing.*

176

Yet each man kills the thing he loves,
By each let this be heard,
Some do it with a bitter look,
Some with a flattering word,
The coward does it with a kiss,
The brave man with a sword!

Oscar Wilde, *The Ballad of Reading Gaol.* Alan Turing quoted this passage to Joan Clarke on the occasion of the dissolution of their engagement. Hodges, *Alan Turing.*

176 ". . . do occasionally practice . . . They're not as savage than they used to be." Alan Turing in a letter to Joan Clarke concerning his arrest. Hodges, *Alan Turing.*

189 "*A philosophical error in Turing's work.* Turing in his 1937 paper, page 250 (1965, page 136), gives an argument which is supposed

to show that mental procedures cannot go beyond mechanical procedures. However, this argument is inconclusive. What Turing disregards completely is the fact that *mind, in its use, is not static, but constantly developing. . . .*" *Some Remarks on the Undecidability Results,* in *Kurt Gödel: Collected Works,* Volume II, *Publications 1938–1974,* ed. Solomon Feferman, John W. Dawson, Jr., Stephen C. Kleene, Gregory H. Moore, Robert M. Solovay, Jean van Heijenoort, (New York: Oxford University Press, 1990).

190 "a Viennese washerwoman type: garrulous, uncultured, strong-willed." Oskar Morgenstern's comments on Adele. Dawson, *Logical Dilemmas.*

192 "I'm so happy to drive without a genius in the car." Adele liked to say this to visitors, especially mathematicians, whenever she drove them home. An anecdote relayed by Dr. Verena Huber-Dyson in *Gödel and the Nature of Mathematical Truth II* (published online at www.edge.org).

193 "awfully charming," Kurt Gödel's description in a family correspondence of a pink flamingo statue Adele placed in the garden of their Princeton home. Dawson, *Logical Dilemmas.*

201 "It is hard to describe what such a conversation . . . means for me: here is one of the most brilliant men of our century, greatly attached to me, . . . [who] is clearly mentally disturbed, suffering from some kind of paranoia, expecting help from me, . . . and I [am] unable to extend it to him. Even while I was mobile and tried to help him . . . I was unable to accomplish anything. . . . [Now,] by clinging to me—and he has nobody else, that is quite clear—he adds to the burden I am carrying." A memorandum by Oskar Morgenstern, Perkins Memorial Library of Duke University. Dawson, *Logical Dilemmas.*

ACKNOWLEDGMENTS

Thank you to Dan Frank, my editor, for his vision and thoughtfulness—and for finding this book with me.

I gratefully acknowledge a Dream Time Fellowship (2003) from the National Endowment for Science, Technology and the Arts in the U.K.

ALSO BY JANNA LEVIN

"Science as it is lived. . . . [Levin's] book is a gift to those people who want to think big but came to a screeching halt about two dozen pages into . . . A Brief History of Time."
—Discover

HOW THE UNIVERSE GOT ITS SPOTS
Diary of a Finite Time in a Finite Space

Is the universe infinite or just really big? With this question, the gifted young cosmologist Janna Levin not only announces the central theme of her intriguing and controversial new book but establishes herself as one of the most direct and unorthodox voices in contemporary science. For even as she sets out to determine how big "really big" may be, Levin gives us an intimate look at the day-to-day life of a globe-trotting physicist, complete with jet lag and romantic disturbances. Nimbly synthesizing geometry, topology, chaos and string theories, Levin shows how the pattern of hot and cold spots left over from the big bang may one day reveal the size and shape of the cosmos. She does so with such originality, lucidity—and even poetry—that *How the Universe Got Its Spots* becomes a thrilling and deeply personal communication between a scientist and the lay reader.

Physics/Cosmology/978-1-4000-3272-3

ANCHOR BOOKS
Available at your local bookstore, or visit
www.randomhouse.com

Printed in the United States
by Baker & Taylor Publisher Services